There's No Surf in Cleveland

There's No Surf in Cleveland

STEPHANIE JONA BUEHLER

CLARION BOOKS · NEW YORK

Clarion Books
a Houghton Mifflin Company imprint
215 Park Avenue South, New York, NY 10003
Text copyright © 1993 by Stephanie Jona Buehler

Printed in the U.S.A.

Library of Congress Cataloging-in-Publication Data
Buehler, Stephanie Jona.
There's no surf in Cleveland / by Stephanie Jona Buehler.
p.   cm.
Summary: Having moved with his mother to Los Angeles after his parents'
divorce, ten-year-old Philip finds that he hates California and does
everything in his power to get back to his relatives in Ohio.
ISBN 0-395-62162-3
[1. Moving, Household—Fiction.   2. Los Angeles (Calif.)—Fiction.
3. Divorce—Fiction.]   I. Title.
PZ7.B8835Th   1993
[Fic]—dc20   92-11981
CIP
AC

VB   10   9   8   7   6   5   4   3   2   1

To my parents for helping me read,
my husband for helping me write,
and my daughter for licking the stamps.

1

My bed shook. My shelves shook. I shook. I jumped out of bed and flung open the door to my bedroom.

"Mom?" I strained to see her in the early morning light.

"Philip, just stay put! It's an earthquake!" Mom shouted from her doorway.

The sight of her pale face, her fingers clutching the door frame, made me gulp. Our eyes locked. We listened to the rumble of the ground, waited for the earth to silence.

I was terrified. It was the same kind of scared I get from one of those dreams where I'm falling and falling and then wake up right before I splat! My heart pounded so hard I looked down and saw the middle button of my pajama top shaking. What a way to start a weekend.

The shaking stopped. I looked at Mom in her cow-boy print pajamas. They usually made me smile, but not this morning.

Mom gave a silly laugh, then blew a puff of air that brushed by her curly brown bangs. "Well, I guess it's official—we're Angelenos."

"Uh-uh. Not me!" I scowled. I had sworn I'd go back to Cleveland the first time the ground shook and that meant *now*.

"Did you hear anything break?" Mom threw a red bathrobe over her pajamas.

"No." How did she expect me to hear anything over the sound of the scream still stifled in my throat?

I followed her into the living room. The sun had begun to shine through a gap in the blinds. Far off I heard a fire siren. I ran to the window and looked out between the slats, expecting to see crumbled buildings and toppled streetlamps. Nothing had budged, not even a blade of grass. I turned away, relieved. Nothing seemed wrecked in the apartment, either. Then I saw Mom kneeling over something on the floor.

"Oh, Philip, look! The picture of Grandma and Grandpa broke." Mom showed me the damage. A crack ran through the glass over my grandparents' smiles.

I felt my lip tremble—I didn't know that lips really did that. I'd had to remind Mom the whole summer after we left Cleveland to buy a frame for that picture.

The apartment floor heaved and fell with a thump. "Oh, no! Not again!" I yelled and ran for the kitchen door frame. The hanging lamp in the dining room swayed—weeek, weeeek, weeeeeek! My stomach swayed with it. I threw my hands up in surrender.

"All right! That's it! I'm not going out to breakfast—I'm going back to Cleveland!" I marched toward the hall closet to get my suitcase, already regretting my dramatics. I had a little problem: no plane ticket, not until Mom got her paycheck on December first, and that was next week. But I was on a roll.

"Don't be ridiculous, Philip. It was just an aftershock." I could hear Mom's feet chasing after me.

"My mother, the seismologist." I pulled my suitcase out of the closet. "I'm serious. Call Grandma and tell her I'll be starting Christmas vacation three weeks early."

"*And miss school?* Put that suitcase away."

"Mom, no. I told you before we left that as soon as there was one little earthquake, I'd be out of here." I put the suitcase on the bed and zipped it open with great ceremony. Boy, it was an ugly case, green and yellow plaid. Jumbo, a stray cat I'd recently befriended, sauntered into the room and jumped up to sniff this monstrosity.

3

"Philip, I mean it. We haven't even been here six months—"

"However long we've been here, it's plenty enough for me." I angrily pulled some shirts off their hangers and lumped them into the suitcase. I grabbed some more shirts and threw them onto the cot I slept on. "Dad didn't even let me keep the four-poster. It's never going to feel like home until we get all our furniture."

Mom groaned. "That bed belonged to your father when I met him—you know he wanted to keep it."

"What a guy." I opened my drawer and pulled out socks. Lots of socks. There's a rule that quantity adds to drama. Jumbo began to sniff again.

"He's still your father."

"Like he cares. He hasn't written me in two months."

Mom fell silent, pushing her fingers up into her short curls. She couldn't help that my father didn't want to be tied to a family. I knew I was giving her a hard time, but face it—there wasn't anybody else around to take my anger out on.

Besides, she was the one who decided to move us to Los Angeles, where my polo shirts and loafers had instantly labeled me as a nerd. I picked up my new running shoes from the floor of the closet and snorted at them. What a waste! I'd never fit in.

I flipped the shoes back onto the floor. Then I felt

Mom's hand on my shoulder. She gently turned me around to face her.

"Maybe your father doesn't contact you as often as he might, but I know he thinks about you." She tried to get me to look her in the eye, but I wouldn't. "Philip, come on. You know he cares. And you know I care, too."

"If you cared, we wouldn't be here." I heard my voice becoming louder and louder. "I could be out by the lake playing football with Chris, or watching Grandma make strudel, instead of rolling around like a marble in a box. If you cared, we would have stayed in Cleveland!"

"That's not true. Look, I thought coming here would be good for you, too. We both had a lot of memories, we both know it was difficult for you after the divorce." Then Mom said firmly, "I thought we were a team."

Some team. The little old Lorsches against the big, big city. She acted like we were going to win. Win what? A piece of fallen plaster? "Yeah, right, Mom. Lorsches, nothing. Los Angeles, six-point-one."

Mom didn't like that remark. She crossed her arms and pursed her lips. "That's not funny."

I ignored her. "Why couldn't we have stayed with Grandma and Grandpa? They didn't mind. They said we could stay as long as we wanted."

"Maybe they did, but I couldn't. I need to be on my own, I want to pursue my career—"

"Oh, yeah, right, a career in the film industry." I pushed my nose up and tilted my head back. "How ever so hip, Mother."

"I don't like that attitude. Hip—pfft. You should know me better than that. I think my knowledge of period furniture will really help me make a contribution to set design. Josh says—"

" 'Josh says'!" I grabbed my throat and gagged. Josh was my mother's boyfriend, a screenwriter who taught at the junior college where Mom worked in the theater arts department office. "Who cares what Josh says?"

Mom blinked angrily at me while she thought, but then her look softened. "Okay, right. Forget Josh. Let's look at you instead. You keep complaining how unfair I've been to you. How about how unfair you've been to me?"

"What?" I grabbed Jumbo for support. Imagine calling me unfair, a boy who feeds stray cats!

"Yes, unfair to me. All you ever do is whine. I can't seem to do my job as a mom right around here because everything I do as far as you're concerned is one big mistake. Like it isn't tough enough being a single parent! Well, let me tell you something!"

Quick! Where was the volume control?

"Getting two people moved halfway across the country and settled into a strange new city is a major accomplishment—especially when one of the two is an uncooperative, unappreciative preadolescent boy who can't see past his own two loafers!"

Jumbo chose that particular moment to jump down and rub against Mom's ankle. Now Mom screamed, "And get this cat out of here!"

I watched Jumbo roll once and shoot out the door. "Come on, Mom. Don't make me put him out. The earthquake probably upset him."

Mom pulled a crumpled tissue from her robe and sniffed into it loudly, which did nothing to muffle her voice. "NOW!"

"Oh, all right." I hurried into the living room, grabbed the cat and put him out in the hallway. Then I put out a bowl of the awful, dry, fishy food I kept hidden behind the Raid in the kitchen cabinet and told the cat not to pee until I could take him outside.

I rushed back into the bedroom. Mom and the suitcase were gone. I looked in the closet again, but there was just a gaping hole where my suitcase had been.

"Mom?" I called.

She opened her bedroom door and glared at me. "You are not getting that suitcase back. You are not leaving Los Angeles. You may be in sixth grade, but you are only ten years old and I am still your mother!"

"But I'm almost eleven. Besides—"

"If you keep complaining, I just might keep you

here over Christmas and you won't go to Cleveland at all."

"Keep me over vacation? No! You wouldn't!"

"Try me."

Something in my head went "Boing!" Mom usually didn't punish me this way. She liked to talk things out. Her bunched up face told me that this was the sign of a desperate mother. But I wasn't ready to give up.

"I've flown by myself before, you know. Twice."

"I know, but that was with my permission. I can't let you go back to Ohio now, Philip. Remember what we've talked about. You've got to learn to adjust, earthquakes and all."

Ugh, that word. "Adjust." Everyone was always worrying about my getting used to things, ever since fourth grade when my dad disappeared for a couple of months after the divorce. He hadn't actually vanished into thin air; he was with his girlfriend somewhere looking for antiques to sell, something Mom hadn't done with him because she wanted to be home with me. Now he was back in Cleveland. It hadn't made me feel any better about the divorce to know that Dad was more interested in hunting down armoires than spending time with me.

In fact, when my parents got divorced it upset me so much that I felt like I was watching Earth through a telescope. I remember one day my teacher offered me a one-way ticket back from planet Snorzik whenever I was ready to join the class. The word "adjust" came up a lot then. I hated that word. Somehow "adjust" went along with "accept," and there were just some things I couldn't accept. Ever. Like Dad disappearing. Like becoming an official Angeleno. Like earthquakes.

"All right, fine, forget it," I spat. "I'll wait for vacation. Except by the time Christmas comes, California will probably be an island and I'll have to swim to get to an airport. But don't worry—I'll 'adjust.' "

Mom responded by pretending to play the violin. In her cowboy pajamas, yet.

"Go ahead, Mom. Laugh. But don't expect me to save you when the roof comes down on our heads."

"Deal," was all she said before closing the bedroom door in my face.

2

"**F**ine," I said to the door. If Mom didn't want me to fly, that was all right. I'd take a bus.

I went to get my money sock out of my dresser drawer and spilled my savings on the bed. My grandparents had sent me some money to make up for being apart at Thanksgiving, so I had sixty-two dollars and nine cents. I did some mental math. After buying Christmas presents and cat food, I'd have exactly zero left.

Maybe I could walk. After all, it was only twenty-five hundred miles to Cleveland. I thought for a moment of asking my pal Washington to lend me his skateboard, but I knew he'd never understand. Washington was a rare breed, a second-generation Angeleno who felt blessed to have been born in what he called Paradise.

Even so, I couldn't say anything bad about him. He was the only real kind of friend I'd made in L.A.

We saw a lot of each other—Washington lived in my building and was in the same class at school. His parents were divorced, too; his father lived in Oregon and his mother worked selling cosmetics in a department store. And we both got help with math after school from the same person, Bernice, who lived downstairs. I knew we'd be friends when we agreed that the chocolate cookies Bernice baked for us tasted like floor tiles.

I went to the bathroom to wash up. I didn't bother to glance in the mirror because I always appear the same—square chin, sandy blond hair, and green eyes like Dad's. My all-American, cornflake-ad looks make people here ask if I'm going to be an actor. It's embarrassing. At those times I make sure I gag real loud and fall on the floor to get my answer across.

I shrugged into my Kent State sweatshirt and a pair of jeans. I opened the hall door. Jumbo looked up in mid-crunch. We took the elevator down from the third floor. The elevator smelled like egg salad. I opened the front door to the building and let Jumbo slip out of my arms. Then I followed him onto the small lawn in front of the Nirvana.

The Nirvana is the name of the apartment building where we live. Mom says Nirvana is where Buddhists who meditate a lot end up if they keep their hearts pure and their noses clean. But I'm sure if the Buddhists saw our Hollywood version of

Nirvana they'd get up off their prayer stools and run screaming into the night. Our building has a kind of red pagoda roof and the entrance is made to look like the doors to a Chinese temple. It's really gaudy. But the cats hang out here, so I figure we must have good garbage.

Jumbo had taken off, but a replacement rambled up to me. "Hi, Caveman." I put my hand out to a gray cat that could have been Jumbo's brother. Caveman allowed me to pet him, and I sat on the grass to tell him my troubles. I don't mean I talked out loud. I'm not that cracked, even from living in Los Angeles. With cats, you see, you can tell them your troubles just by touching them. They seem to look at you with just the right amount of sympathy. Sure enough, as I rubbed the cat's neck he rolled over puppy-style and gave me a slit-eyed look of understanding.

"Hi! Did you feel the temblor this morning?"

I looked up to see Washington standing over me. He was wearing camouflage hightops. They clashed with his shirt, on which golden pineapples floated in a blue sky. With his dark skin and his oversized skateboard planted next to him like a surfboard, he almost looked Samoan.

"A trembler?" I asked.

Washington frowned. "Not trembler, temblor. A small shake. The guy on the radio said it was only a three-point-one."

It bothered me that Washington was so casual, like he'd been shaken in a million quakes that hadn't bothered him a bit.

"Only a three-point-one," I mimicked. I decided to match his attitude. "Anyway, I didn't even feel it."

"You lie!" He chucked me lightly on the shoulder. I fell over on the grass like a wounded man. "What happened to you? Did something fall on your head in the quake?"

"Naw." I lay out flat on the lawn. Caveman crawled onto my stomach and purred. "I just can't figure out why anyone would want to live where you can't even count on the earth holding still."

"Oh, no. Don't get started on that 'I hate L.A.' stuff again."

"Well, look at it." I raised my arms up to the sky. "It must be eighty degrees today."

"Isn't it great?" Washington lay down next to me and looked up. "If I didn't have chores to do I'd be skateboarding at the Venice Boardwalk right now. Hey, why don't you relax and enjoy the sun?"

"I'd rather eat snake lips."

"Blue skies, bright sun, big white clouds floating over the ocean . . ."

"But it was just Thanksgiving! Winter's supposed to be cold. I hate this place. It's hot and I'm sweating. I don't know why anyone—Washington?" Washington had started snoring. Big, ugly snorts.

"Washington! Wake up! Wake up! C'mon. I've got a problem."

I sent the cat on its way and gave Washington a shove. He lifted his head and blinked, then pretended to rub the gum out of his eyes.

"Listen to me," I went on. "You can laugh all you want, but I'm serious. I want to go back to Cleveland. I mean it. Now. Today."

"Do what?"

"I want to take the bus back to Cleveland. I've traveled by myself before. It's not that big a deal. There's just one little problem—no money." I wiped the sweat off my upper lip. I really hated L.A.

"You mean run away?"

"Going to my grandmother's isn't exactly running away."

"Are you coming back?"

"I guess." I shrugged. Actually, I hadn't thought that far ahead.

The glugging sound of a large car motor made me look up the street. I'd have known that old avocado green-gold Cadillac Coupe de Ville convertible anywhere. It belonged to Josh, my mother's boyfriend. I looked back at Washington and groaned.

"Great. It wasn't bad enough to be woken up by an earthquake. I have to go out to breakfast with Mom and Josh today."

"I don't think Josh is so bad. He has that really cool turquoise buckle on his belt. And he's smart."

14

"You think so? How would you like to stand in for me?"

"Somehow I don't think that would work," Washington mumbled.

We watched Josh park his topless green whale and then walk up the street towards us. Josh wore flannel shirts and had a beard. I only understood about half of what he said whenever he spoke to me. Not that I paid much attention. Mom said he was deep, but I thought he was dumb.

Mom met him in the theater arts office her first day on the job. He'd had one of his screenplays produced, but it was a big flop. Mom says he doesn't like to talk about it. I guess he teaches at the college so he can eat.

"Hi, Philip, Washington." Josh looked down at us with his thumbs looped by his belt. He had on a new pair of wine-colored cowboy boots. Where else would anyone seriously wear cowboy boots, especially that color? As far as I could tell, there wasn't a horse around for thirty miles. "Ready for breakfast?"

"I guess." I stood up and brushed the grass off my rear.

"Washington, are you coming with us?"

"No, sir. I'd better get home. I have a bunch of stuff to do if I want to get an allowance this week." As if on cue, his mother appeared at the door of our building. Washington had never said she was strict, but she *looked* strict. She always wore all-black dresses and red lipstick. My mom tried to get away with wearing something as close to pajamas as possible and no make-up at all.

Washington got up and waved to his mother. He had grass cuttings stuck all over him. "See you later, Phil. Oh, and just keep thinking palm trees."

3

"**W**hat does that mean?" Josh asked as we walked into the Nirvana.

"I don't know. Something to do with Hollyweird." I pressed the button for the elevator.

"Are you hungry this morning?"

I hadn't even thought about breakfast. Earthquakes are very distracting. But eating didn't seem like a bad idea. "Sort of."

"That was some shake, huh?" We got on the elevator. It smelled like stewed fruit. "Did anything break at your place?"

"Just a picture." I changed the subject. "Where are we eating?"

"The Pancake Palace," Josh said as we got out. Like it was some big deal. Mom and I had gone to the Pancake Palace a couple of times after we first moved to L.A., when she was really tired and broke. As Mom said, at least the plates were clean.

Josh gave Mom a kiss when she greeted us at the door. That was okay. I had gotten used to guys kissing my mom after the divorce.

Mom turned her motherly eye on me. "Philip, is that how you're dressing to go out to breakfast?"

I looked down at my sweatshirt. So it had a few stains on it. I lied, "It was just washed."

"Never mind." Mom dropped it. She didn't like to argue with me in front of Josh. Okay, so there was one advantage to having him around.

Mom put on a sweater. Not that she needed it. She wasn't used to warm weather in fall, either. We left the apartment, rode down in the fruit-scented elevator, and drove off in Josh's cavernous car.

The restaurant was pretty empty, probably because clean dishes weren't a big enough attraction to get people out on a Saturday morning. Josh stays up late at night to write and gets up late, too. I stared at my menu.

"What'll you have?" the waitress asked. She was young but she had on these weird old-lady glasses with rhinestones on the pointy corners.

"I'll have the el cheapo breakfast plate, eggs scrambled," I said, slapping the menu shut.

Mom glared at me for a microsecond, then looked at the waitress. "The *special*, please. Poached eggs, wheat toast, no butter, and decaf. I have to make up for the goat cheese pizza we ate last night—the one Philip wouldn't even touch."

"That was a good pizza, but you're not kidding about the calories. I'll have the same special," Josh said, "with butter on the side."

"Three specials, then." The waitress pushed up her glasses and left.

There was a pile of change in the ashtray. The waitress must have forgotten to pick up her tip. I hated it when a waitress did that. It was like she was testing the honesty of her customers. The coins were just too tempting to pick up and put in one's pocket. Especially when one wanted money for a ticket to Cleveland. I started playing with the coins.

Suddenly Josh plucked a quarter out from under my hand.

"Do you like magic?" He began rolling the quarter over and under the tops of his knuckles.

"Let me try that," I said.

But Josh made me wait. Mom and I watched while Josh showed how to make the coin swim between his knuckles. Then he held his hand up in the air, waved it, and snapped it open. The quarter was gone. I had expected that, but I was a sucker for magic.

"How did you do that?" I wanted to know.

"With a little prestidigitation."

"I know, but how?"

"If I show you, do you promise not to tell? That's the magician's code, you know."

I nodded my head like the Boy Scout I had never been. I watched a few times as Josh explained what he did with the coin. I picked up another quarter from the ashtray and tried it.

"It worked! Did you see, Mom?"

"Now I see it, now I don't," she joked lamely.

To my humiliation, my quarter rolled out from between my fingers and clanked onto the table. "Oooops."

"No, no, no, no. That's not the way you make it reappear. We have to work on your presentation." Like a Spanish dancer flipping a fan, Josh flicked open his hand and revealed the original quarter. "Ya, ta, dah!"

I practiced the trick with Josh until our el cheapo eats showed up.

"Hey, I thought I had a bigger tip here!" yapped the spectacled waitress. "Did you guys get so hungry you ate it?"

She tried to sound playful, but I could tell she was a little annoyed, too. Mom looked away, embarrassed.

Josh laughed, also embarrassed, and handed the woman the quarter he had been using. But I had to get dramatic.

"Here's another one, right here." I showed her my empty hand. Then, imitating Josh, I waved my hand. At the last moment I decided to add my own magic word. I opened my hand with great aplomb and yelled, "Gnaddenhutten! Here you go, ma'am."

She chuckled and put our breakfast on the table. "That's a pretty good trick. How do you do that?"

I shook my head. "Sorry, but I have been sworn to secrecy. Here, take your quarter."

She pushed up her glasses and smiled. "No, that's okay. Keep it."

"All *right!*" I pushed the quarter into my pocket. It was the easiest money I'd ever made. And it gave me an idea.

"You know, have you ever thought about getting him an agent?" the waitress asked Mom.

I went into my special act—gagging and falling over in the booth. But carefully. I didn't want to lose that quarter.

4

"**B**oys! What are you doing?" Mrs. Trundle looked up from the math group she was working with to yell at us.

"Nothing." I don't have to tell you that that wasn't true. In fact, what I was doing was giving Washington a little lesson of my own on how to do Josh's magic trick. But Mrs. Trundle continued to stare, waiting. "I was just asking Washington if this was a trapezoid or a parallelogram."

"Very interesting, since the assignment I gave you was on circles. Since neither one of you is a math genius, the next time I look up I'd better see you working."

We looked at each other, silently agreeing to ignore her. If she wanted cooperative learning, this was as good as it got. I went back to teaching Washington how to palm a coin.

"That's it! You've got it!" I mouthed a cheer. I

thought a moment. "Why don't we do the trick at lunch?"

"What do you mean? What for?"

"We could ask kids for a quarter so we can do the trick. We'll make the coins disappear and I'll keep them to buy my ticket."

"Isn't that stealing?" Washington said so loudly I almost clamped a hand over his mouth.

"Holy moley, keep your voice down!" I shouted in a whisper.

"Sorry," Washington whispered back. "Well, isn't it?"

"No, it's entertainment," I explained. My voice had a higher pitch in it than I intended.

"Why are you so anxious, Philip? You're getting on my nerves."

"Don't you get it? I have nightmares about earthquakes. Every time someone walks by the desk and the floor shakes, I'm ready to take a dive."

Washington whistled softly and tweaked the sleeves of his flamingo-decked shirt. "Boy, you are in bad shape."

"I am, I really am. Look, I'll give you a ten percent cut of whatever we make." Washington gave me a look that said he wasn't going to go for it. "Okay," I said, "fifteen percent, but you have to help bring in business."

Washington's eyes brightened. "Okay, then. Sure, I can always use money around holiday time."

"Good. Let's shake." Then I looked up to check out Mrs. Trundle. She saw me and twisted her bright pink mouth, then looked at her watch.

"All right, everybody. It's time for lunch. Put your books away and line up quietly."

We walked to the cafeteria with the military precision Mrs. Trundle demanded. My teacher in Cleveland thought that lines were stupid and let us walk out in a group if we were quiet. But then, a lot of things here at Sierra Bonita Street School were different from those at Elm Street School in Cleveland. While we had a lot of black students and even a family from India at Elm Street, nothing could have prepared me for a school filled with people from so many places. At Elm Street I was part of the crowd, but at Sierra Bonita I was a minority student—a plain vanilla, bland, middle American.

As our line moved I rubbed the top of my head, remembering how a group of Hispanic kindergartners had come up to me my first day of school in L.A., jumping and pointing at my light-colored hair. It wasn't easy being different. I sighed as I stared at the back of Jorge's neck.

"What are we having for lunch today?" Ariel screamed over to the people from our class coming out of the other side of the cafeteria. Ariel had come to L.A. from Israel a year ago but spoke fluent English already.

"Chalupas," Chi Long called out.

"Cha-who's?" I questioned Jorge. Whatever they were, they had to be a whole lot different from the Cambodian food Chi Long ate at home.

"A chalupa is like a tostada, but you hold it in your hand," Jorge explained.

"What's a tostada?"

Jorge groaned and stepped ahead in line. "Do you even know what a taco is?"

"I've had a few," I countered. Only once, but I wasn't about to admit it.

"A chalupa's like that, then, only opened flat."

"Oh, I get it," I said.

"About time," Jorge mumbled.

As I stared again at the back of Jorge's neck, I thought of the Mexican restaurant in Cleveland where everything tasted like burnt chili powder. The cafeteria's version wasn't much better, but I didn't really care for any sort of Mexican food. I wished that my mother still made my lunch for me like she did when I was little—cheese singles on wheat bread, sandwich cookies, and an apple. I guess I could have made my own lunch, but I probably would have been teased for my lack of culinary imagination. Still, I found myself longing for a cafeteria that served boiled hamburgers or hot dogs—safe, bland, middle American food.

I picked up my lunch tray and milk and walked over to the class's lunch tables under a eucalyptus tree. There were musty eucalyptus berries that the

25

squirrels had chewed and dropped all over the place.

"Eww! Eww!" Carmelita squealed as Washington brushed off the table, sending berries flying everywhere.

"Madam," Washington said with a bow, then pointed to a clean seat.

"Thank you, sir." Carmelita curtsied, then turned and started chatting in Spanish with Soraya.

Washington and I sat down. He leaned over and whispered in my ear. "Carmelita's nice to everyone. Why don't you try the quarter trick on her first?"

I put down my fork and took a deep breath. I wasn't exactly the most popular guy in the class, since I had only been in the school a couple of months. Plus I only spoke one language—no Spanish, Vietnamese, Korean, Armenian, or anything else. But I wanted that money. I wanted to go back to Cleveland.

I tapped Carmelita on the shoulder. "Do you have a quarter?"

Carmelita looked at me and frowned, her dark brows coming together over her dark eyes. "Why?"

"I want to show you a trick. A magic trick."

Carmelita and Soraya shrugged at each other. Carmelita dug around in one of those clear plastic purses the girls all seemed to have. She found a quarter and handed it to me.

"Watch!" I commanded. I was surprised when the whole table looked up at me from their lunch trays. I flicked my wrist and gave a clap.

"Gnaddenhutten!" I opened my palm. The quarter was gone.

"Wow!" Carmelita gasped.

"How'd you do that?" Alexander asked.

"Give me a quarter and I'll show you," I told him. Alexander, a Japanese-American boy, could get away with bringing his lunch because he brought his noodle-y meal in a stack of black lacquered boxes instead of a paper bag and ate his food with chopsticks. He laid his utensils on a chopstick rest and fished in the little square pocket of his Levi's. I'd never seen anyone use that little pocket before. Then again, before this September I'd never seen anyone bring chopsticks to school, either.

"Gnaddenhutten!" I shouted again. Then I got really brave. I walked over to the other side of the table and pretended to pluck the quarter out of Alexander's ear.

Alexander laughed. Several kids called out, "Do mine! Do mine!"

"Can I keep the quarter?" I asked Alexander.

"I guess. Sure," he answered good-naturedly. I dropped the coin into my pocket. I gave a nod to Washington to get busy with the people on his side of the table. Pretty soon the entire sixth grade had gathered around us. We made quarter after quarter disappear, all right. Disappear right into our pockets.

"Uh, oh. Here comes trouble," Washington muttered.

I looked away from Jorge, expecting to see Mr. Alvarez, the noon aide, or worse, Mrs. Donavan, the principal. All I saw was the usual bunch of kids on the yard.

"Miguel," Washington whispered.

Before I had a chance to ask, a boy pushed Jorge aside and stepped in front of me. "Let me see! How do you do that?"

"Hey, Miguel, no fair! It's my turn next!" Jorge protested.

"Not if I don't say so." Miguel looked me in the eye and demanded, "Show me how you do it."

I wasn't going to argue with someone about six inches taller and thirty pounds heavier than me who had a head as big as a school clock. "Give me a quarter and I'll show you."

Miguel pulled out a coin and handed it to me. I hid the quarter, pulled it out from behind Miguel's ear, then hid it again.

"That's pretty neat," he said grudgingly. "But I said to show me."

"I did show you."

"Show me again."

"Give me another quarter."

Miguel scowled, but he stuck his hand in his pocket and pulled out a nickel and a dime. "Here, take the nickel."

I shook my head. Maybe being stubborn with someone like Miguel was stupid, but no one was going to shortchange me. This was too important. "It has to be a quarter."

Miguel mumbled something that I was sure he'd get in trouble for saying if he said it out loud. But he finally did manage to part with the coin I wanted.

"Now show me." Miguel put the quarter firmly into my palm. I repeated the trick.

"Wait a minute—I didn't learn anything."

"You didn't say to *teach* you—you just said to *show* you."

"Oh, come on. You know what I meant."

"I can't. I promised someone I wouldn't. Magician's code of honor." I had taught Washington the trick, but that was another story.

"You promised—I'm sure," Miguel sneered. He came pretty close to tapping my chest with his finger, then pulled back. It was a weird gesture, something I would expect an adult to do, not someone my age. I flinched as he clenched his fist. "Give me back my money."

"No! Why should I?" I felt I had to stand firm, even if my knees were shaking.

"Because I lent you the money, I didn't give it to you. Now give it back."

29

Behind Miguel I could see Washington signaling for me to do as he had said. I ignored him.

"I said I'd *show* you. My 'show' costs a quarter."

"Give me back my quarter!"

"Do it, Philip," Jorge pleaded.

"Do it!" yelled Soraya.

"You little dweeb! I'm going to mash your brains!" Now Miguel raised his fist. I started to duck, but a boy behind Miguel grabbed his arm just before he lunged. Miguel pushed his friend's hand away as Mr. Alvarez rushed over. He glared at us both like we were two insects deserving extermination.

"What's the problem here, Miguel?"

"Nothing," I heard myself answering. I wasn't so dumb I'd get Miguel in trouble for threatening to mash my brains. If I did, he might end up mashing my entire body.

The lunch bell rang. Saved.

"Behave, boys." Mr. Alvarez's warning finger pointed at Miguel alone. He turned away and blew his whistle. "All right, line up!"

"You're dead meat, Philip," Miguel growled. "Dead meat."

I suddenly found myself wondering how I'd look sporting a sesame seed bun. Not that I really wanted to find out.

5

"**W**ould you quit looking for Miguel? We haven't seen him since Monday." Washington sounded exasperated.

"I'm not looking for him," I told Washington. Which was a lie. I peered over my shoulder again. The word *nirvana* took on a whole new meaning as I hurried my step toward home. "Come on, Washington, I want to count my quarters." Washington, wearing a dark green shirt decked with pink orchids, raced out ahead of me, then I raced out ahead of him, and so we raced back and forth until we reached home.

Wilson greeted us on the lawn in front. I picked him up and nuzzled his neck. He smelled like truck grease, but I didn't mind. I needed a cat, even if all I got was a mouthful of fur when I kissed its fuzzy head.

"Open the door for me," I called to Washington.

The elevator smelled like cigar smoke. Washington tapped on Bernice's door. Bernice's two dachshunds, Ping and Pong, yelped, "Arf! Woof! Arf! Woof!" one after the other.

Bernice opened the door. She was wearing slippers made to look like Clark Bars and a Garfield T-shirt that came to her knees. She worked all night as a bookkeeper for a nearby hotel and she always looked like she was ready for bed when we saw her. But she did a pretty good job tutoring me in the math I missed while visiting planet Snorzik.

"Boy, you two sure made it home fast." She stood aside to let us in and looked at the cat I held. The dachshunds looked, too, their tails twitching like mad. "Who's that?"

"Wilson."

She closed the door and looked at him closely. "Ugh, he's all dirty."

"I know. He must have been under a car or something."

"You and your strays. He'll get my furniture filthy." It was hard to believe that Bernice had never noticed that the furniture she rented from the Nirvana was already dingy.

"Can I at least take him upstairs and feed him first? I worry about what they eat outside."

"Please," she begged. "Wait! Take a cookie before you go." Bernice gave us each a chocolate floor tile and we left.

I hauled Wilson up to my apartment. Washington flopped onto the white wicker couch Mom had brought from Cleveland while I fed Wilson some dry food on a paper plate. I sat down on a white wicker chair. We ate our cookies, pretending we needed to aid our jaws to chew up and down. The apartment was filled with crunch music.

"Let's count our money," I said with my mouth full. I pushed aside the morning mess of newspaper Mom had left on the white wicker coffee table. Then I pulled the quarters out of my pockets. They made an awful clatter on the glass. "Hurry, or Bernice will come up here to get us."

Washington added his coins to the pile, and we began making little four-quarter-high stacks of the coins we had collected so far during recess and lunch. In the end we had ten piles. Washington and I both whistled.

"This is unbelievable," Washington gasped. "How much of that is mine?"

"A dollar," I said firmly. What did I know? I was even worse at math than Washington.

"Are you sure?" Washington looked at me and frowned. "Do you mind if I check it on paper?"

"Be my guest."

Then he grabbed a pencil and an envelope that was left on the table. "What was that shortcut Bernice taught us? Let's see, ten percent of ten dollars—one, oh, oh, oh." Washington wrote his numbers carefully. "Cross out the last oh and that leaves a dollar, right? Now, the other five percent . . ."

"Can't we just make it a dollar? My brain hurts." I pulled a flowered cushion over my head.

"No, we can't. A deal's a deal." Washington's eyebrows shot up. "Hey, I just figured out the rest. I'm going to take another two quarters."

"Fine, take them," I agreed. "Anything. Just no more math, okay?"

"Deal," Washington said. He counted out six quarters and put them in his pocket.

"How much more do you think I need to buy a ticket?" I asked him.

"I don't know, but I think the plane's pretty expensive. Anyway, I always take the bus when I go to visit my Dad. Why don't you call Greyhound?"

"Good idea. Let me hide this first." I ran into my room and came back with my old money sock. Washington helped me pour coins into the toe. I raced back to my room and stuck the sock into my sacred underwear drawer as I tried to do some quick mental math: $8.50 + $62.09 = wow! I came back out wiping my sweaty palms on my pants. It was the most money I'd ever had that Mom hadn't put into a savings account.

Washington watched as I took out the yellow pages and looked under Bus Lines, then dialed. I listened to a polite recording, then some Christmas music. I started singing along. Washington joined in on the chorus of "Jingle Bells."

A woman's voice broke into the song. "Season's greetings—how may I help you?"

"Oh, uh." I cleared my throat, embarrassed to have been caught yowling carols. "How much is it to Cleveland one way?"

"Well, we have several different fares. Do you know which one you want?"

"I'm not sure. I just want to visit my grandparents."

She laughed. "How old are you?"

"Ten, almost eleven."

"Okay, then, hold on." I heard the computer click and beep. "Ninety-eight-fifty one way."

"You mean ninety-eight dollars and fifty cents?"

"That's correct. Do you wish to put in your reservation today?"

"No, not today. Boy, I'm going to have to come up with some real magic to get that kind of money."

"All right. Be sure to call us when you do."

"I will. Merry Christmas." I hung up and turned to Washington. He had turned his eyelids inside out. "Stop that! That's disgusting!" Washington blinked to turn the lids back to normal. "Well, I guess you heard how much it costs."

"Yeah." Washington tch'd and patted greasy Wilson. "Yuck. Listen, Philip, maybe you should just wait and take the plane."

" 'Maybe you should wait'! Wait for what? Wait for Miguel to make me into ground round? Wait for California to become an island in the Pacific? Wait for snow to fall in Los Angeles?"

"What's snow good for, anyway?"

"Good for? To walk in, to run in, to ski in, to sled in." I flopped into the wicker chair again and shook my head. What's snow good for! "Besides, snow is beautiful."

"Not as beautiful as me in my shades, riding my board down by the beach. Some day soon I'm going to get a real surfboard, too. Who needs skis?"

I gave up. I'd had this talk too many times before with other people in L.A., not just Washington. None of them ever understood the good side of snow.

"We'd better get back to Bernice's and do our homework. Maybe she knows some shortcuts for memorizing those geometry definitions." I picked up Wilson and held the door open. We got into the elevator, which smelled like onion bagels. "Do you think we can make another thirty dollars by the weekend?"

"That's an awful lot of people, maybe the whole school. I still think you should wait." My face must have looked pretty sad because he chucked me on the shoulder and said, "Okay, okay, we can start on the third graders tomorrow."

"You think? But what about Miguel? What if he comes up to bother us again?"

"Quit worrying. We'll just go behind the work shed."

"You mean where the janitor keeps his stuff? That's not a bad idea." I opened the door to the building and let Wilson out. I spotted Jumbo, sunning himself in the window of an apartment across the street. Very loyal, cat. "I thought we weren't supposed to go behind the shed."

"We aren't. But that's never stopped anyone before." We rode the elevator back to Bernice's floor. This time we let ourselves in and the dogs ran up quietly to sniff us.

"Where were you guys?" Bernice asked casually.

"I just finished putting the cat outside," I told her. "What do you know about circles?"

"Radius, circumference, diameter. Are you with me so far? No? Here, let me see your assignment." We sat next to Bernice on the couch and did our homework and ate floor tiles until someone knocked at the door. I looked up, curious, since it was too early for Mom to come get me.

"Arf!"

"Woof!"

"Arf!"

"Woof!"

"Ping! Pong! Quiet!" Bernice opened the door. I was disappointed to see Josh poke his head in.

"Hi, Bernice, Washington. Get your things, Philip. Your mom and I left the campus early today."

"Okay." I got my backpack. At the door I looked over my shoulder and gave Washington a thumbs-up sign. "See you tomorrow."

Washington wiggled his fingers over his other cupped hand like a magician conjuring up a rabbit. "Don't get into any hocus pocus."

"Not without an assistant," I said, and grinned.

6

"**W**hat was that about?" Josh asked me in the hallway.

"Nothing." No way would I tell Josh about the fortune Washington and I had gained through his dumb magic trick.

"Oh. Well, did you have a good day in school?"

"It was okay." I took a whiff of elevator air. Moo goo gai pan. My mouth watered. "It smells good in here. For a change."

"I'm glad you think so, because I believe that smell is our dinner."

"Chinese takeout? Great!" I tore out of the elevator ahead of Josh.

The door to our apartment was open. I headed straight for the dinner table. Steam rose out of the little square boxes Mom had already lined up. I started to open one a little more for a peek.

"Philip! Go wash your hands first," Mom called, wiping her hands on a dish cloth.

I was back in record time to join Mom and Josh at the table. I looked in all the containers. "Oh, boy. Almond duck, egg rolls, spare ribs. What's in these boxes? Moo goo gai pan, shrimp fried rice, chow mein, and noodles." I looked up in a panic. "Almond cookies?"

"And fortune cookies, both," Mom assured me.

"What would you like, Amy?" Josh asked.

"Just a little rice and some moo goo gai pan. Those chiles rellenos we ate at lunch today probably raised my cholesterol several points." Mom's comment was a joke. Beneath the droopy clothing she usually wore, Mom was slim. Unlike Mom, I intended to pig out on the only ethnic food I willingly allowed to pass my lips. I eagerly took the carton of vegetables from Josh when he passed it to me.

"How was school today?" she asked just as I shoveled a forkful of fried rice into my mouth.

"Skoo?" came my muffled response. I'd spent so much energy on fund-raising I'd almost forgotten such a place existed.

"Yes, school." Then she began to drill me. "What did you learn? Do you have homework? Any papers for me to sign? Any disasters to report?"

"Disasters!" I sputtered rice on the table and began to cough.

"What is it? What happened?" Mom held my teacup out for me to take a drink, but I had managed to recover on my own. "What's wrong?"

"I have a memo from school to give you. About earthquake preparedness." I wiped my hands and pulled from my pocket a pink paper I had folded into one-inch squares. I smoothed it out carefully and handed it to Mom. "We're having an earthquake drill, too. The whole school has to pretend a major quake has hit the city."

Mom twisted her mouth at Josh as she took the memo, then became serious as she studied the list of items to have on hand in case of an earthquake. She ran a finger over her upper lip and looked up.

"Actually, we have most of these items. Blankets, canned food, flashlight, extra batteries. We even have things in the car from Cleveland in case of a blizzard—remember?" She put the paper on the table. "Anyway, there's nothing to be done about a natural disaster, except to be prepared."

"But I'm not prepared, Mom." I pointed to the ceiling. "You know, all it'll take is one good shake to bring down the Nirvana on our heads. I don't know about you, but I'm not ready to die!"

Mom and Josh looked at each other. Josh kept his chopsticks still. Mom laid her fork down.

"We're at dinner, Philip." Mom was trying to control herself, but she sounded irritated. "I bought all this food as a treat for you. Can we please keep the conversation pleasant?"

"Fine. Just don't look at me when the Nirvana caves in and we have nothing to eat but a tablespoon of peanut butter."

Mom took a sharp breath. "You know, Josh and I didn't have to stop at Shanghai—"

Josh put his chopsticks to his lips to stop Mom. "So, Philip, are you excited about your trip back to Cleveland?"

"You had better believe it." The thought of my hidden stash of coins and the possibility of a bus ride made my appetite return. I speared a spare rib. "I hope it's snowing."

"You *like* the snow?"

Here we go again. "Sure. Don't you?"

"I've never really been in it. I got stuck in a little surprise flurry once when I drove through Utah, but that's all." He looked across the table at my mother and raised one eyebrow. "Speaking of bad weather, I sure hope it doesn't rain all the way up the coast. It can be wet this time of year."

"Coast? What coast?" I asked. I looked at Mom, then at Josh, then back at Mom. No, it couldn't be. They couldn't be going away together while I was visiting my grandparents in Ohio. "Who's going up the coast?"

Then things got strange. Mom started choking on *her* rice. I'd never seen anyone down a cup of tea so quickly.

"Ooops," Josh said softly while he watched.

"What's the matter? What's going on?" I tried to pretend I hadn't figured it out so I could watch them squirm instead of doing the squirming myself. I grabbed a handful of chow mein noodles and stuffed them into my face.

"Well, you see, your mother and I . . ." Josh began.

Mom shook her head at Josh. "Please, let me. Philip, Josh and I are going to drive up to Monterey over Christmas while you're away."

I had been right, but I swallowed hard anyway. A chow mein noodle stuck in my throat like a fish hook. "Well, that's certainly a surprise, isn't it?"

"I was going to tell you tonight after dinner."

"Philip, it isn't as though your mom and I started dating last week," Josh put in. "We've even talked about getting—"

"I'm full." I let my fork clang onto my plate. "I've lost my appetite."

"Fine." Mom pushed herself away from the table. "Josh, would you help me clean up, please?"

Josh took my plate away and went over to stand next to Mom at the kitchen sink. When he came back from the kitchen, he didn't look at me. "I've got some writing I want to do at home tonight. Talk to you all later. 'Bye, Amy. Philip." The front door closed quietly.

"Too bad," I sneered as I smashed a piece of rice into the tablecloth with my finger. I felt Mom

43

watching me and waited for her to tell me to stop playing with the food.

Instead she sat down across from me and said softly, "I'm sorry, Philip. I had planned on sitting down with you tonight and telling you about the trip Josh and I are going to take while you're visiting Grandma. I guess the dinner was supposed to put you in a good mood."

"Gee, that was really swell of you. Anyway, it didn't work."

"I can see that. Forgive me for not being perfect."

I flicked a piece of rice onto the carpet by mistake, then let it sit there. "Why?"

"Why what?"

"Why are you going away with some guy you hardly know?" So I sounded slightly hysterical. Who wouldn't be?

"Philip, that's not exactly true. Josh and I haven't known each other long, but sometimes feelings grow quickly. I'm sorry he sprang it on you. He isn't a parent and he's not used to dealing with kids. That probably sounds like an excuse, but I'm sure he didn't mean to hurt you."

"What difference does it make how I'm told, anyway? No one really cares what I think around here."

I looked up, surprised to find Mom's eyes filled with concern. She leaned over the table. "Why are you so angry that I'm going away? No, wait, that's the wrong approach." She gave a little wave and started over. "Okay, Philip. I'm listening. Tell me what you think."

I looked down at the table again. I felt angry and kind of embarrassed that my mother was taking a trip up the coast with a man. I couldn't bring myself to discuss it aloud.

"I don't know," I said finally. "I'm not sure. I'm confused, I guess."

"I can understand that. Do you want to know what I think?" Mom asked gently. I didn't answer. She put her hand over mine. "I think Josh is the nicest man I ever met. I love him a lot."

"Do you love him as much as—" I stopped.

"As much as what? As you?"

"No, not that. I know that." I looked up at her. "As much as you loved Dad when you married him?"

Mom sighed and closed her eyes. It was a sigh I knew I'd never understand. "It's different, Philip. I loved your dad when I met him. Now I love Josh."

We sat quietly for a few minutes. Then I said in almost a whisper, "I'm glad then, I guess." Glad, and sad.

"If you're glad, I'm glad." Mom leaned over and gave me the squishy kind of hug that was still okay to get. "Which reminds me—you haven't said a word about your Christmas present this year. What would you like?"

I figured Mom was still feeling guilty about her

trip, so I decided to try my luck. "A permanent cat."

"Forget it," she replied firmly.

"I've got it! Let me miss the earthquake drill. Just thinking about earthquakes makes me sick."

"Oh, Philip. Anyway, give your gift some thought over the next few days."

"I'll do that." But I knew I wouldn't come up with anything better.

7

The next morning Mrs. Trundle divided us into groups to talk about the holiday party. Everybody said that was one good thing about being in Mrs. Trundle's class—she let her class plan their own party. But as I listened to her dividing us into committees, I felt smug because I didn't plan on being around for the party. I'd be in Cleveland if I had anything to do with it. After doing magic all week, I had made almost twenty dollars.

"All right, then," Mrs. Trundle directed. "Go to your groups and begin discussing what you would like to do for the party."

We scraped our chairs along the floor as we scrambled to get to our assigned tables. I found myself at Table 3 with Washington, Jorge, Christine, Emma, and Bob.

"Hi." I plunked into my chair. Christine and

Emma were already talking in a language I didn't recognize.

I must have had a puzzled look on my face because Washington said, "Tagalog."

"Tagalog?" I asked slowly. I'd never heard of it. "Where's Tagalogia?"

Christine and Emma stopped talking and looked at me. Once again I felt like an alien in my own country. Christine spoke. "We're not from Tagalogia, we're from the Philippines."

"Oh. Sorry." How had Washington known that? I was about to say more but Jorge crooked his finger for me to come closer. "What?" I asked him.

"I hear Miguel was looking for you this morning," he muttered.

"Still?" I bugged my eyes. "I didn't see him at all today, or yesterday, either. I was sort of hoping he had moved or something."

Washington had leaned in close. "So? Did he say what he's going to do to us?" he asked.

I tugged on Washington's sleeve to shut him up as Mrs. Trundle clicked over to us in her heels. Washington sat up straighter.

"I think we ought to have grapefruit juice, don't you?" I said, loud enough for Mrs. Trundle to hear.

"Oh, yes," said Christine.

" 'Fer sure,' " drawled Bob.

"My fave," Jorge chimed in.

Satisfied that we were busily planning the party,

Mrs. Trundle clicked away. Washington relaxed into his chair in a posture which suited someone wearing a shirt covered with hula girls.

"Yuck, grapefruit juice." Christine squirmed in her chair. She translated to Emma.

Emma made a sour face even I understood. "Yuck!" Then she and Christine went back to their own conversation.

"So?" Washington said again.

"So he says he's going to push Philip's face through a mile of broken glass," Jorge reported.

"Are you stoking me?" Bob said eagerly. I couldn't understand his stupid California surfer slang, but he sounded like he couldn't wait to see it happen.

"Oh, well, if that's all he told you," I said sarcastically. What, me scared? Yes, but I had reason to be. Mom was a pacifist. She didn't believe in war, between countries or between people. She'd never hit me, and she'd tried to teach me to talk my way out of problems. But somehow I didn't think Miguel would speak my language. Guys like Miguel spoke with their hands. Punching people out just wasn't in Mom's bag of mom tricks.

"Just let him near me. I'll show him some real trouble," Washington bragged as he made a muscle with his arm.

"Wrong," I said.

"Why? What are you going to do?"

"I don't know. I'll just walk away if he threatens me, I guess."

Bob laughed, then looked under the desk at my feet. "You'd better put jets on your running shoes, dude. Hey, pretty awesome! When did you bag your nerd shoes?"

"And what has Table Three planned so far?" I waited for someone in our group to answer. The rest of them just sat there, looking like a gang of mouth-breathers. Now the whole class was waiting.

Christine and Emma exchanged worried looks. I had no idea what they had been talking about, but judging from their faces it hadn't been about the party. I grabbed the blank paper and pretended to read it over.

"Let's see," I bluffed. "We thought we could swap Christmas ornaments. Everyone brings an orna-ment, and we put them all into a bag, and then everyone gets to pick out a new one to take home."

I was surprised when the class started buzzing ex-citedly about the idea. Actually, we had done an or-nament swap last year in Cleveland. I had ended up with a really stupid-looking reindeer.

Mrs. Trundle pulled the long face that meant she was impressed. "Table One, what did you come up with?"

Chi Long shrugged and whispered, "Sing Christ-mas carols?"

"Big deal!"

"Really original!"

Everyone laughed.

"All right, enough. Table Two, what about you?"

They looked up from a huddle and Soraya said, "We like Table Three's idea best."

"Yeah, us too," Chi Long agreed.

"Okay, what about Table Four?"

An Armenian boy named Akapek sheepishly held up another blank paper.

"Oh, well." By now Mrs. Trundle sounded strained. She looked at Table 5. "Bouy?"

"Which boy?" Alexander asked.

"You know which Bouy!" A Cambodian girl at the table gave him a good-natured sock in the arm. "Me!" I admired her for taking teasing so lightly. Somehow I never managed to do that. Bouy continued, "We liked the ornament exchange, but Ariel also said she could bring some dreidels and teach us a game."

"Great idea! What does the class think?" Several students nodded their heads in agreement. "Then it's settled—dreidels and an ornament exchange." Mrs. Trundle glanced at the clock. "Tomorrow we'll plan refreshments. Put your chairs back and line up for lunch."

"Thanks," Christine whispered behind me in the cafeteria line.

"No problem."

Washington and I scarfed down our beef-and-bean burritos to make time for our noon magic performance. I kept watching for Miguel. I spotted him at one of the fourth grade lunch tables trying to get a burrito away from one of the boys. At least he wasn't bothering us.

"Come on, let's go for some fifth graders today." Washington jabbed me in the ribs, then belched and tossed out his paper lunch tray. I followed him over to the first fifth grade table.

He walked up to a small black boy wearing a Dodgers T-shirt. "Hey, Blue, how's it going?"

"Not so good since the series ended. I can't wait for spring."

"I know what you mean. Hey, do you want to see a magic trick? I'll need a quarter."

"Not especially," Blue answered. I knew that the fifth graders would be a tougher crowd to sell than the third graders.

Washington crossed his arms and rocked back and forth on his heels. "What's the matter, don't you have any money?"

"I've got plenty—for video games."

"You're still playing those? Won't anyone let you play their Nintendo?"

"Sure they will."

"Then you don't need a quarter."

"Gee, I didn't think about it that way." Blue felt in his pocket but came up empty-handed. "I don't have a quarter." I couldn't believe anyone could be so dense, but then Blue grinned and nudged the boy next to him. "Hey, Greg! You got a quarter I can have?"

"Sure."

Washington took Greg's quarter and waved his hands. He had obviously been working on his technique. "Hocus pocus!"

Blue rolled his eyes, but he looked surprised when Washington flipped his hands open and the quarter was gone.

"Wow, that was quick. Do it again." This time Blue pulled out his own quarter—Aha! I thought— and gave it to Washington.

"Wait a minute!" Greg shrieked.

"Ah, it's just a quarter. Watch my friend here." Washington pushed me out in front of him. "He's even better."

A crowd—no, a gold mine—gathered around us.

"Come on, everybody, let's go behind the shed," Washington called. "We can have a regular show back there."

Washington made Blue a lookout while I called out the word "Gnaddenhutten!" over and over again. I couldn't believe how everyone wanted to keep seeing the trick done with *their* quarter.

Miguel stayed away, but he kept sending his spies: All the most grisly students at the school kept peeking around the shed. It was a little like being watched by vultures. But they never bothered us, and when the lunch bell rang we strutted back to class, our pockets full of jingling coins. Talk about heavy metal.

My eyes met Miguel's when we lined up after the lunch bell. He gave me a hard look. And then he grinned.

I'd seen a grin like that before. On a shark.

I would have spent the afternoon worrying, but Mrs. Trundle had a monster math assignment on the board when we got back to class. I had been working for about fifteen minutes when Mrs. Trundle waved a note in the air and called, "Philip, Washington! Mrs. Donavan wants to see you both right away!"

"The principal!" I gasped.

"No, the zoo keeper," someone piped. The class laughed.

Mrs. Trundle ignored them. "Get going. Now!"

As if we had a choice.

8

As we scuttled across the yard I felt like an insect about to meet up with a can of Raid. I burped up burrito. "Now what?" I asked Washington. I couldn't even guess. I'd only been to the principal's office once before—in Cleveland, when I was all upset after my dad disappeared. I had a feeling this was not going to be the same kind of trip.

"What do you think?" Washington asked in disgust. "We're in trouble."

"Why?"

"Why do you think? All those quarters!"

"How do you think she found out?" I pestered.

"How do *you* think?"

"Stop that. Listen. Do you think it was Miguel?"

Washington gave me a sharp look. "No—Santa Claus."

"What do you think is going to happen to us?"

"Just what you think will happen." Washington

shook his head. "Boy, I don't know who's dumber—you for coming up with such a stupid scam or me for listening. One thing for sure, we're about to get our ears fried."

"You mean she's going to yell?"

"Only if she's mad."

"So what do I do if she asks us anything?"

"Just do what I do," he said. I felt better until we got to the office and he let out a shaky sigh.

The office manager stopped typing and pointed a red-tipped finger at us. "Mrs. Donavan is waiting for you."

All the women in the office followed us with their eyes as we walked behind the counter to Mrs. Donavan's door. I felt like I was already shackled and being led off to a cell.

"Washington. And you must be Philip. Have a seat, boys." Mrs. Donavan showed us two hard chairs in front of her desk. The door clicked shut behind us. Mrs. Donavan twirled a pencil in her hands as she looked us in the eye, one after the other.

That's when I noticed the bracelets. Big, thick gold chains circled her wrists. At the circus I went to in Cleveland the ringmaster wore bracelets like that. Anyone who wore chains that thick could probably get me to jump through a hoop.

"Tell me what you know about the two boys who stole quarters from the fifth graders at lunch today."

The bracelets jingled like the coins we had collected as she shook her pencil at us. But she wasn't yelling. She just used that soft, controlled voice that people in charge sometimes use to show that they are truly superior.

Why does it always feel worse when you expect someone to yell, and then they speak quietly? I didn't know what to say. I looked to Washington for guidance. He was gazing at the green walls like an archaeologist studying hieroglyphics. So I did the same, pretending to see something very interesting on the window blinds.

Suddenly Mrs. Donavan whacked her pencil on the desk. I jumped a mile in my chair and heard Washington gulp.

"I'm waiting, boys!"

But Washington just found a blister to pick at on his palm. He was *cool!* I looked at my own unmarked hand with equal fascination.

"Boys! I want to know NOW! Who was stealing from the fifth graders?"

"But we weren't stealing!" I blurted.

Washington smacked his palm to his forehead and groaned. "Oh, Lorsch. You're such a wimp."

"Quiet!" she commanded, then she narrowed her eyes. "What do you mean, 'not stealing'?"

"Because we gave them a magic trick for a quarter. It was an even trade."

"Oh, you think so? I happen to know that several

57

students expected to get their quarters back afterwards, but did not. I call that stealing. What do you call it?"

For the first time in my life I actually wrung my hands. Not only did the principal think what we had done was dishonest, but that cheese-brain Miguel must have ratted on me. It had to have been him! He was the only kid who thought we had stolen anything. One dissatisfied customer in the whole bunch, and he complains to management. I now understood why I liked cats so much—it was a dog-eat-dog world.

"I said, what do you two boys have to say for yourselves?"

"We're sorry," Washington mumbled without enthusiasm.

"What? I can't hear you," she hissed.

Washington sat up and blinked fast a couple of times. "I said I'm sorry for stealing, Mrs. Donavan."

"Me, too," I chimed in. "I mean, I'm sorry for stealing, Mrs. Donavan."

Mrs. Donavan twirled her pencil again. Her bracelets jangled. I didn't dare say that I thought making an honest quarter was admirable for a simple midwestern boy in the sixth grade.

"At one time I enjoyed magic, too, you know," she said.

Washington and I exchanged puzzled looks. Then

I brightened. Maybe we had touched a warm place in Mrs. Donavan's heart after all.

"But I never used my tricks for selfish purposes, like you two." My smile faded as fast as milk from a cat's whiskers. "I never cheated anyone. I did a show each Saturday for the kids on my block, and I gave the money I made to a local hospital."

I looked over at Washington again, but his head was bowed in shame. I bowed mine too.

"I understand today was not the first time you took quarters."

"Yes, Mrs. Donavan. That's right," Washington told her.

"What did you boys do with the money?"

"Most of it is at home," I admitted. Washington was right—I was a wimp.

"Ideally, boys, you should return every quarter you took, but I'm afraid that would take too much class time and cause too much chaos. Instead, I'm going to talk to your mothers about giving the money to the school sports fund. We could use some new volleyballs."

"Yes, Mrs. Donavan."

There went my bus ticket, along with my vision of Cleveland covered with snow. If I was stuck in L.A., it was a sure bet that any day now California would break clean away from the mainland like a square off a bar of Hershey's chocolate. With nuts, of course. I had to keep myself from grinning at my own joke.

Mrs. Donavan opened her desk and pulled out an official-looking pad of forms. "I want you to know you could be suspended for what you did, but since this is your first infraction I'm only going to ask to see your mothers here tomorrow before you're allowed into class."

I watched Mrs. Donavan's braceleted hand move as she wrote. I knew how hurt Mom was going to be when I told her about my venture. She'd get that funny pinched-nostril look of hers that I hated. I burped burrito again. She wasn't going to be too thrilled about coming to see the principal before going to work, either. I wondered what my punishment would be.

Then I had a terrible thought. What if Mom didn't let me go to Cleveland? What if she kept me locked up during Christmas vacation? What if I ended up with no Christmas at all? In my mind's eye, I saw a pathetic pile of gifts. A box of brown socks and a small kazoo.

"You may return to class now." Mrs. Donavan handed us each a note. "And from now on, boys, try to use your talents to benefit others instead of yourselves."

9

"**S**tealing! How could you do such a thing?"
Mom shook Mrs. Donavan's note in my face. Just as
I feared, her nostrils were pinched. She was so
angry, I could hardly look at her.

"I had this plan—"

"*But why, Philip?*" I guess Mom wasn't ready to
listen yet. I didn't blame her. "Why did you steal?
You knew I was going to give you spending money
for your trip."

"I know. But I—"

"Taking from others what doesn't belong to
you—that's not the way I brought you up!" She
shook the note at me again. "I want an explanation
right now."

"I've been trying, Mom. I'll tell you. It started
after the earthquake." So I told her all about how
badly I wanted to go back to Ohio, and how I got the
idea for the trick from Josh, and how Washington

61

and I entertained the third graders behind the shed. My gut told me not to say anything about Miguel, though. That's all I needed, for Mom to go to the principal and complain about his bullying me.

"Anyway, I guess somebody told Mrs. Donavan," I wound up. "She called us in and yelled at us. You should have heard her, Mom." Mom just looked at me with her gray eyes. I sighed. "Anyway, she said we had to give all the money we made to buy volley-balls for the school."

Mom bobbed her head. "I think that's an excellent idea. How much did you make?"

"Seventeen dollars and twenty-five cents, less Washington's cut."

"Seventeen dollars! Philip, how could you?" Mom was mad all over again.

"I still don't have the bus fare to Cleveland."

"How could you possibly think I'd let you ride twenty-five hundred miles on a bus by yourself?"

"I told you, I'm not two years old. I could handle it."

"Judging from your behavior I'd have to disagree. Philip, you still don't realize that you *stole*."

"That's the part nobody gets. It wasn't stealing, Mom. It was entertainment," I explained again. "Most of the kids seemed to understand that. Even the second graders understood that."

"The second graders! What? You stole from them, too? How much?"

"Just a dollar or two."

"That's still a lot of money to take from seven-year-olds. Where is the money?"

"In a drawer."

"Go get it right now." Mom groaned and rubbed her forehead. "I guess I'm going to be late to work tomorrow on top of everything else."

I walked to my room and got my sock. I still wasn't sure Washington and I had stolen anything. Sometimes adults make such a big deal over things. A kid would make it simpler. There wouldn't be a long discussion. A kid would say something like, "Hey, you did something dumb!" I'd think it over, and if I agreed, then maybe I'd fix it. Or maybe I'd just walk around for the rest of my life knowing I'd done something dumb and that would be punishment enough.

I came back with my sockful of change and emptied it on the table in front of Mom. "I still don't get why it's stealing."

Mom pressed her lips together as she studied me. "You really don't understand, do you?"

"No, I don't. We did a trick for a quarter, that's all."

"Here," she said, slapping a quarter from my pile into my palm. "Pretend I'm a student and show me what you did."

"Let's see, how did I start? Okay, I'd come up to you and ask if you wanted to see a magic trick. Then you'd say all right, and then—" A glitch in my story made me stop, but I wasn't sure what it was, so I went on. "Then I'd ask you for a quarter."

"Ask me."

"If you want to see the trick, I need a quarter."

"What if I don't have a quarter?" Mom asked, closing her hand.

"Then you don't get to see the trick."

"Well, I want to see the trick, so I'll give you my quarter."

I took the coin from her and performed the trick I had practiced to perfection. I held up my empty hand and cried, "Gnaddenhutten!"

"Very good. Now where's my quarter?"

"It's gone. Vanished." I wasn't sure if I was supposed to act proud or not. "Want to see it again?"

"No, I don't. And you took my only quarter! You never told me you were going to keep it!"

"I never—what?"

"Said you were going to keep the money before you did the trick. I didn't find out until afterwards that my quarter was going to belong to you. I don't think that's right, do you?"

I thought over what had just happened for a moment. She had a point—I never did say what I intended to do with the money. "Maybe you're right. I guess I did kind of cheat. I didn't mean to, though. I thought we were doing a neat trick."

"You know what? I believe you." Mom squeezed my hand. "But it's still wrong."

"I know. I'm really sorry." I squeezed back. Then I realized Mom hadn't said anything about punishment yet. I started to panic. "Can I still go to Cleveland?"

"Yes, but I'm going to cut your spending money in half. And no TV for a week. And don't ever do anything like this again!" Then she tch'd. "I wish you weren't in such a hurry to leave Los Angeles."

"And I don't know why you had to pick a place where the ground isn't even safe to stand on."

"It isn't safe anywhere, honey. Maybe you don't remember, but there were tornadoes every spring in Ohio, not to mention blizzards every winter."

"Well, at least I *felt* safe there."

"Of course you felt safe. You grew up there. You had a lot of friends. And your grandparents were there."

"I miss them," I said, sniffing back the beginnings of some tears. I felt like crying, but the events of the day had taken too much energy out of me already.

"I'm sure."

I gave a final sniff and put my chin in my hand. "And I miss the trees turning color in fall. I miss Grandma making hot chocolate after school. I miss her chocolate chip cookies. The ones Bernice bakes taste like floor tiles."

"That's not nice. Anyway, is it really so bad here?"

"Yes," I said flatly. Why didn't she believe me?

"Tell me, then, what's so awful about having the sun out all the time, and a beach nearby to walk on, and lots of fresh vegetables all year round?"

"I hate to break this to you, Mom, but it's going to take a lot more than broccoli to change my mind."

"Because you had your mind all made up to hate it here before we ever even left Cleveland."

"And when we got here it turned out that I wasn't all that wrong. Los Angeles is weird."

"Different, not weird." Mom sighed. She stood up and wiped her palms on the tail of her oversized pink shirt. "Someday you'll learn to accept that the only thing certain in life is change."

Accept! Adjust! I clenched my teeth and growled. I snarled and clawed at the air. I jumped up and down. But Mom didn't hear. She had already walked into the kitchen, leaving me alone. To think. That was Mom's idea of a trick. Unlike mine, her tricks usually worked.

I stopped ranting and took some deep breaths to calm down. I walked over to the window and looked out. One light after another came on in the buildings up and down the street as day turned into night. Why? Why couldn't things just stay the same? I tried to think of something, anything, that didn't change in some manner. Rocks wear away, stars become black holes. Parents get divorced, people move. But

I still wasn't convinced it had to be that way. There had to be some magic, some trick I needed to learn, to keep things as I wanted them to be.

I needed to see one of "my" cats. "Mom?" I called out. "I left something down at Bernice's. I'll be back in a sec."

"Okay, but hurry—dinner will be ready soon."

I went to my bedroom to get an unopened box of food and one of the paper plates I hadn't had time to hide from Mom and went outside. But there wasn't a cat to be seen anywhere. I shook the box and waited. Nothing. No response, not a single meow.

"Jumbo! Caveman!" I hurried over and peeked around the corner of the building near the trash cans. "Petunia?"

Still no cats. What was I going to do? Who in this crazy city was going to listen to my troubles and take them seriously? I walked to the garbage cans by the side of the building. I didn't see any cats, so I held my nose and lifted the lid to the dumpster. All the garbage had been collected. The cats must have gone after a better class of garbage.

What ever made me think I could keep a stray? What good were they, anyway? Even Jumbo wasn't around to pay attention to me, the cad. I felt lonesome as I turned and walked back into the Nirvana.

10

Going to see Mrs. Donavan with my mother wasn't nearly as bad as I'd feared. First of all, Mrs. Donavan wasn't wearing those monster bracelets. Second of all, she and Mom mostly ignored me as they discussed my lack of adjustment to my surroundings.

What was worse than listening to them talk was having to leave my money on Mrs. Donavan's desk. At least I had time to put all the quarters into a ziplock bag. It would have been embarrassing to leave my stained, worn sock on the principal's desk. The sock was safe at home with my original funds still stashed in the toe.

When I finally got out to the yard that morning, I was relieved to see Washington smile at me. He walked up and asked, "Did you get chewed out last night?"

"What do you think? Did you get in trouble?"

"Yep. Mom said I have to wear a plain T-shirt every day for a week," Washington said, plucking the white one he was wearing. My jaw dropped. What a weird punishment! Then Washington chucked me on the shoulder. "You sucker! I'm just kidding. She won't let me rent any videos until our vacation. What about you?"

"No TV for a week. Not even the Nature Channel. And she cut the spending money she was going to give me for my trip in half."

"How are you going to have fun in a place like Cleveland without any money?"

I didn't feel like arguing. Sure, there were parts of Cleveland that were, well, unattractive. But in Ohio there were all kinds of trees and flowers that didn't grow in California. Cleveland also had fluffy white clouds rolling in the sky most days. I found fluffy clouds especially reassuring. Clouds made only rare appearances in Los Angeles, unlike the ever-present smog which sometimes got so bad my eyes watered. I looked up at the sky. Blue, with the usual band of brown haze choking the horizon. Not a cloud in sight. Boring.

"What are you looking at?" Washington asked.

"Somebody's idea of a perfect day."

"You're weird." The bell rang. "Come on, let's line up."

I followed behind Washington. Suddenly he put his arm out to stop me.

"Wait, Philip. There's Miguel."

As before, I looked over to the other sixth grade line. My eyes locked with my enemy's. I looked away first. I couldn't help it. I turned around, pretending I had just wanted to talk to Washington.

"You know what really gets me? All he lost was two lousy quarters, and we ended up in the principal's office."

"Tell me about it," Washington agreed.

"You guys! Shhhh!" Christine warned us.

Our class was quieter than usual all morning. At first I thought it might have something to do with the fact that they had two minor criminals in their midst. But when I got to my seat and began to work, I realized that once again I had managed to forget the earthquake drill. It was scheduled for that afternoon at exactly 1:05 P.M. I stopped working on my report on African wildlife, put my face into the T-for-Tiger volume of the encyclopedia, and groaned.

"What's up, dude?" Bob asked.

I sat up. "Do I look sick?"

"No, why?"

"Never mind." Too bad. A trip to the nurse could have saved me from the perils of earthquake preparedness. I sat holding my pencil over my paper for a minute or more. Then I poked Bob with the eraser. "Are you sure I look okay?"

"I told you, yes. Anyway, you know Mrs. Trundle doesn't send anyone to the nurse unless they throw up or have head lice. If you cop, she's just going to tell you to put your head on the desk."

Normally the lunch bell signaled relief, but today it only meant we were one step closer to practicing for our doom. We lined up, then stood and waited for our cafeteria lunches.

"It's cold out," Soraya complained.

I almost laughed aloud. It was 65 or so but all the kids were rubbing their arms like they were standing naked in the snow. Angelenos were really wimpy about the cold.

"What are we having?" Washington asked.

"Chalupas," Chi Long answered.

"Again?" I whined, but no one joined me. Maybe everyone was too busy staying warm. And it *was* warm. Sixteen more days, I consoled myself, and I'd be out of here.

I picked up my cardboard tray from the cafeteria rail. Chalupas, corn-off-the-cob, and applesauce. Whatever happened to grilled cheese? As I walked out the door I could just hear my mom's voice saying, "Oh, Philip, don't be so *narrow*." Mom's idea of a great meal was anything with sun-dried tomatoes. She thought bland was a crime. And I was bland.

I was considering the appearance of my chalupa, which looked like a little tortilla hat topped with lettuce, when someone stepped right in front of me. I came to a dead halt and looked up into Miguel's face.

Neither one of us said anything. My breath started coming out all shaky and my heart began to pound. I felt humiliated, but I couldn't help it. I just had this picture of me in the nurse's office, blood all over my shirt.

But, hey. If he carried out his threat, at least then I wouldn't have to be in the earthquake drill.

"Hey, Lorsch, what's it like for a wimp like you to end up in Donavan's office?"

One of Miguel's pals laughed right behind me. I knew better than to turn around and look.

"No big deal. Mrs. Donavan is all right," I said, still looking at Miguel.

Miguel cracked up. He had really white, really big teeth. Suddenly I found myself thinking about the photos of tigers I'd been looking at in class. Miguel continued to laugh. What could I do? I tried laughing, too. The instant I opened my mouth, he stopped.

"Come on, Miguel," I heard myself saying. "You got off easy. I went to the principal's office. All you lost was fifty cents."

"Hey, that wasn't my fifty cents. It belonged to my cousin. And my cousin is really angry."

"For fifty cents?" I felt my eyes blinking fast. " 'Fraid that's not my problem."

"What did you say?" He came a step closer.

I moved a step back. "I said it's not my problem if you were dumb enough—"

Miguel made a fist. I couldn't run with my tray, so I just kept backing up. Just as he swung, it felt like someone tripped me from behind. I went down like a fifty-pound bag of kitty litter.

Flinging away my food tray, I scrambled to sit up again. Shredded lettuce hung from my eyelashes. Applesauce dripped from my chin. I had corn kernels in both ears. My OSU sweatshirt was splattered with taco sauce. And the chalupa made a stunning hat, I'm sure.

I looked up to see Mr. Alvarez. He shouted over all the laughter, "Hey, Miguel, leave this kid alone!"

"I didn't do nothing." Miguel threw his arms out to his sides as he looked down at me, slob of the day.

"Is this true?"

I flicked away a piece of lettuce and stared up at Miguel. He actually looked afraid. I gloated. I had him just where he had wanted me.

"I told you, Miguel," said Mr. Alvarez. "One more fight on the yard and you're suspended."

"I didn't do nothing, I said," Miguel yelled. "He just fell over, that's all. Right? *Right?*"

I didn't say anything. I wanted to wait and see what Mr. Alvarez would do to Miguel.

"I saw you swing, Miguel," Ariel said.

"That's not true!" one of Miguel's spies called out.

"All right, come on. Let's go to the office and talk it over with Mrs. Donavan. You, too. Get up . . . ?"

"Philip." I stood and brushed off my poor, pained rear.

"Tell him," Miguel pleaded. "Come on, man. Look, I'm sorry you fell. I'm sorry."

I heard several boys muttering behind me now. They were probably in shock that Miguel apologized to anyone. Two things entered my mind. First, I couldn't be absolutely sure I was tripped. Second, I really didn't want to see Mrs. Donavan again.

"He's right," I told the yard teacher. "I slipped on some lettuce. It's my own fault. Walking and talking. It's too much for me."

"You're not trying to protect him?"

"No, why should I? I'm not afraid of him."

Knowing Miguel was scared of getting in trouble, I could afford to be brave.

"All right, then, Philip. Why don't you go get another tray? And you—stay out of trouble." The aide turned, blew his whistle and ran off to give grief to someone else.

Then I did something truly dumb. I put my hand out to shake on a truce with Miguel. I waited, then felt like an idiot as Miguel stared at my hand.

"What's this? I'm not shaking your hand, Lorsch. You're still dead meat," Miguel growled. I watched him run off to the basketball court.

What really bugged me as I limped back to the cafeteria was that I knew the day wasn't about to get any better. The temperature had risen even higher.

My smelly sweatshirt stuck to me. I walked out with a fresh tray and looked down at my chalupa. I know, I know, there are children starving in other countries, but that didn't stop me from throwing my lunch in the trash.

One thing I had been right about—things definitely got worse.

11

At 1:00, Mrs. Trundle finished our math lesson and assigned a couple of pages of problems. At 1:02, we all pretended to be hard at work. At 1:03, a soft chatter went through the room. At 1:04, the class became so quiet I could hear a fly buzzing near the chalkboard. At 1:05, one long earthquake bell rang out. We dove to the ground beneath our desks like soldiers hitting the dirt.

"DROP!" the teacher bellowed. It came almost as an afterthought as she joined us on the floor under her own desk.

The bell continued to ring. I cupped my hands over the back of my neck—flimsy protection from the glass and chunks of ceiling that were supposed to fly in a real quake. It was cramped under the desk. I could smell taco sauce on Bob's breath. I tried to concentrate on the wooden floor and its years of ground-in dirt.

Just when I thought my nose could hold no more dust, another short bell rang to tell us that the pretend earthquake was over at last. Now we had to clear out of the building that was pretending to crumble. Everyone began to scramble toward the door in a mock panic. I hung back, hating myself for being the only wienie in the class. My head felt woozy as I thought back on the real earthquake that had rocked me. On top of that, everybody else was bravely goofing around while all I could do was try to cover up my fear.

"That must have been a one-point-zero on the Richter scale," Washington whispered.

"No talking!" Mrs. Trundle shrieked at Washington as we walked to our drill area on the yard. "What if this was a real earthquake?"

Washington looked at Jorge and mouthed a silent laugh. Wash was definitely the wrong person to look to for sympathy. This drill had me convinced that a 7.5 earthquake had just hit the city. How could anyone joke?

Mrs. Trundle told us to sit on the ground in a line and wait. Then she left with a "sweep team" of teachers. The team, Mrs. Trundle had explained, was to check the school for the injured and the dead. I shivered.

I looked around at my classmates. It seemed to me that only a few kids had the right spirit—the pale ones rubbing their arms like fever victims. They were probably rubbing away the cold even though it was about seventy-five degrees out now.

Everybody began getting restless. Some kids were yakking away about what they were getting for Christmas. Elena and Chavela were pegging each other's legs with little bits of gravel. Bob was doing and undoing the Velcro on his shoes, obviously bored. Washington was practicing a dance step on the ground with his fingers to a tune he hummed.

"How can everyone be so casual?" I wanted to scream. "Don't you know an earthquake is serious business?"

Then I caught sight of Miguel. He was studying my sweatshirt with a sneer. Stupidly I looked down. I'd forgotten I was covered with greasy, red chalupa stains.

Miguel poked the boy next to him and whispered, then laughed. Mr. Connors told them to be quiet. Good, I thought. Then Miguel made a rude gesture at Mr. Connors's back. Miguel was brave. Dumb, but brave.

Mrs. Trundle and Mr. McAbbott came out of the main building now, giving support to a girl hopping on one leg. The girl wore a sign, BROKEN LEG.

"Hey, Gretel!" Bob called. "At least you survived!"

Then another student came out on his own from one of the bungalows—single pink stucco classrooms around the edges of the schoolyard. He was having a hoot pretending his arm was in great pain. His sign read BROKEN ARM. Both kids were left with Mrs. Everly, the short round nurse with round black glasses.

The sun felt hot. Wouldn't we ever go back to our rooms? I pulled out the collar of my sweatshirt to let some cool air in.

That's when a tiny pebble hit me on the back of the head. I didn't have to look up to know who threw it. I tried to remember what Mom had said about Mahatma Gandhi's courage as another pebble bounced off my head. Then my stomach growled. Maybe I should have eaten my lunch after all. Except that I actually felt kind of nauseous.

Thwack! A small rock hit the side of my face, close to my eye. But there was no way I was going to be a jerk like Miguel and tell on him the way he told on me.

My stomach growled again. Sweat dribbled down my sides. With most of the teachers on sweep, the commotion on the yard grew worse. Kindergartners began to cry for their mommies. Funny thing—I knew exactly how they felt.

Then something happened I wasn't at all prepared for. Two fourth grade teachers came out from behind the bungalows carrying a student on a stretcher. I looked for the injury sign. There, in

small black letters on a big white card, was the word
CORPSE.

The crowd of "injured" now parted as the two teachers carried the stretcher over to the nurse.

"Hey, look, there's a dead body!"

"Oh, gross."

"Disgusting."

"Can we go home now?"

"I'm going to lose my lunch."

"Me, too."

It seemed like everyone was talking at once. That's when my breathing started getting funny.

"Huuh! Huuh! Huuh!" Maybe it was the smog. I tried to catch my breath but couldn't. "Huuh! Huuh!"

"Hey, what's wrong with you?" Jorge turned around and gave me a funny look.

"I don't—huuh! huuh!—know—huuh! I can't— huuh!—I can't—huuh! Breathe!" I tried again to take in one good deep breath but that only seemed to make things worse.

Washington came over and crouched next to me. "Are you okay? What's the matter?"

"No—huuh! huuuh!" I felt like I had perpetual hiccups.

Washington ran off. He returned with Mrs. Everly.

"Calm down, now. You're just hyperventilating." Mrs. Everly shoved a paper bag over my nose. "Now

I want you to breathe slowly and steadily. That's it—breathe!"

The bag buckled in and puffed out over my nose. And then, at last, my breathing slowed. I felt my brain actually become lighter for an instant. I took the one long, deep breath I needed, then waved the paper bag away.

"Thanks. I'm—I'm all right." I suddenly noticed a crowd of students gawking at me.

Mrs. Everly felt my forehead out of habit. "Good, let's go back to the station."

I pictured myself being led away in front of the whole school like a wounded man, just for breathing funny. They'd put a sign around my neck, AFRAID OF EARTHQUAKES.

"No, really. I'm all right."

"Come on, now, get up. I just want to watch you for a little bit."

"But . . . but . . ."

Then she plucked me up off the ground like a mama bird plucking up a worm. She held onto my arm as she led me away.

"Hey, you forgot his sign," Miguel called. " 'Chicken'!"

"Quiet!" Mr. Connors barked.

Miguel just laughed.

Feeling glum, I joined the other earthquake "casualties." As far as I could tell, I was the only real victim that day, and nothing had even happened. If

81

there ever was another real earthquake, I'd lose it completely.

And to think that only this morning I imagined I could survive the sixteen days I had left in L.A.

Would I ever get back home, to Cleveland?

12

The next sixteen days zipped by, filled with studying for midyear tests, preparing for the class party, making holiday cards, and rehearsing for the winter program in the school auditorium. I saw a lot of dumb stuff about winter in L.A.—fourth graders who had never seen a snowflake sang "Marshmallow World," Mrs. Trundle talked about ingredients for wassail during our eighty-degree weather, fake snow was sprayed onto classroom windows—but I was able to keep my mouth shut. Somehow knowing that I would soon land in the middle of a real winter made the imitation product easier to take.

"I made it! I made it!" I screamed as I hurtled out of the school gate on the last day. I stopped short and turned to look for Washington. I wasn't happy to see him walking across the yard as if it were made out of glue. "Hurry up, Washington! Let's go home!"

Washington finally caught up just as a girl I didn't know pointed at me and whispered to a friend as they passed. That sort of thing had happened so often after the earthquake drill that by now I was able to ignore it. But Washington noticed and asked, "What's their problem? Just because you fainted—"

"I didn't faint, I hyperventilated." Then, to change the subject, I faked a belch and said, "I think I ate too many cookies at the party today. And that punch was gross."

"You mean that orange stuff? Yeah. The ornament exchange turned out good, though." Washington dug in his pocket and held up a clear disk with a unicorn punched into it. It was plastic, so it didn't exactly glitter in the sun, but it was pretty neat anyway.

"I'm jealous," I said. "It was my idea, and look what I ended up with." I held up the ornament I had gotten, a homemade job. Someone had taken a silver dollar shell and glued a blob of green glitter into the center. "Whoever thought of putting seashells on a Christmas tree?"

"Someone who lives near the ocean, like us," Washington said matter-of-factly.

Don't remind me, I wanted to say.

We rounded the corner and the pagoda roof of the Nirvana came into view. I gave a little snort of relief. For the last two weeks I had been nervous about the possibility of Miguel following me home. I felt even better when I saw my newest stray, Petunia, hiding in the bushes in front of the building. I coaxed the white cat out, gave her pink ears a tickle, and plopped down on the lawn. Washington crouched down next to me.

"I guess I'm not being shipped back to Cleveland on a meat tray after all," I said.

"What do you mean?"

"What do you mean, what do I mean? Miguel. He's left me alone all week."

"Didn't I tell you? I heard someone saying today that he had gone back to Mexico."

"Forever and ever?" Hope beyond hope. "I hope he stays down there for good."

"Philip, stop being an idiot. It has to be hard for someone like Miguel to keep going back and forth between here and Mexico. How would you like it?"

I blinked up at him in disbelief. "Why the sympathy?"

Washington shrugged. "I don't know. I think it would be tough to come here and have to learn a whole new language. I'd like to see you try to learn Spanish sometime."

"Why are you defending Miguel all of a sudden? I thought you were on my side."

"I am. But I'm telling you that you're not the only one in this city with problems."

"You mean, I need to adjust."

"Well, I wouldn't have put it that way, but yeah."

That did it. I scrambled up and dashed into the building, sending Petunia running back into the bushes. Washington caught the front door before it closed in his face. We rode the elevator up in silence, breathing in bananas.

Bernice opened the door when we knocked and Ping and Pong skittered into the hall. She was wearing a T-shirt with "Samurai Feline" written on it underneath a cat in a kimono doing a kung fu kick. I shuddered. People certainly had some weird visions of cats.

"Hi, guys, come in," Bernice said brightly. "I know you're leaving tomorrow, Philip, so I baked you my best chocolate chip-banana-peanut butter cookies."

"Gee, thanks," I said in the most sincere voice I could muster. If nothing else I could use the cookies as emergency rations in case the plane crashed. I put down my books and poured a glass of milk for myself. I grudgingly asked Washington if he wanted a glass, too. He nodded and I set a glass on the table in front of him.

I took a cookie off the plate and bit into it. I couldn't believe it. "Hey, this is really good! Bernice, these are great!"

"I'm glad." Bernice beamed.

I decided the good cookies were a good omen for

my trip. I looked over at Washington to see how he liked them. But he was still scowling under a milk moustache.

"What's wrong with you?" I asked him.

"I still don't understand why you're so crazy to leave L.A." Washington sounded upset, but then he grinned. "Did I ever tell you about the time my mom took me to Baltimore to visit a cousin? We went back at Christmas when I was little. All I remember is putting on and taking off a lot of clothes every time we went out. Hurt my tailbone on the ice a few times, too."

"So? So you remember the rotten part of winter," I said defensively. "I just remember the good stuff."

Washington looked away and took another cookie. "Good stuff like what? Icicles hanging off your nose?"

"No. Like going outside and making maple syrup snowcones when the snow is fresh," I replied, starting in on another cookie myself.

"Big deal," Washington snapped. "You get to freeze your buns off at the same time."

"At least there aren't any earthquakes!"

"Just blizzards," he reminded me. "Do you think you'll need a paper bag to breathe for those, too?"

"Low blow, Wash," I said softly. Wouldn't anyone ever let me forget the earthquake drill?

"Sorry." I could tell he meant it. Washington

smiled and pointed his hand with the cookie at me. "Just remember, while you're shoveling I'll be sunning. Tell you what—I'll send you a postcard."

"Why? Afraid I'll forget you?" I mockingly clasped my hands together and held them to my heart. Washington laughed.

"You're a dweeb, Philip." He shook his head and started munching at last. "I guess you have a lot of friends back there you're going to see."

"Yeah."

"It's going to get kind of boring around here."

"At least it'll be Christmas in a week."

"Right, Christmas," Washington snorted. "It'll be a weird one not seeing my dad."

"Why aren't you seeing your dad this year?" I asked.

"He's getting married again, and he didn't think it was a good time for me to meet his fiancée."

"Oh." I didn't know what to say about his father to make him feel better, but I felt I had to say something. "Washington?"

"What?"

"Thanks for trying to help me out with the magic and all. It didn't work, but thanks."

Washington snickered and bobbed his head. "No problem."

I licked chocolate crumbs off my fingers. "You know, there are three things I'm really going to miss."

"Yeah, what?"

"My cats, my mom, and if she keeps baking like this, Bernice's cookies."

"Hey, what about me?"

"Yeah, well."

"Philip! You are so sweet!" Bernice had been listening without my knowing. She came over and hugged me. "I'm going to miss you too, little guy."

"It's only for two weeks." I looked at Washington and sighed. Boy, I wished I was on that plane already!

13

When Mom and Josh finally came to pick me up from Bernice's apartment, I whizzed down the hall ahead of them. I wanted to start packing for my trip. I couldn't believe that my wait had ended, that it was really just a matter of hours before I got on a plane headed for home.

"Whew! It smells like brussels sprouts," Josh remarked as we got out of the elevator on our floor.

"I didn't notice." One more thing I wouldn't have to think about during vacation—stinky apartment elevators.

"Where's the fire?" Mom asked.

"I just have so much to do. I've got to pack and everything."

"And everything!" Mom laughed and let us into the apartment.

I threw my book bag into my bedroom and started for the hall closet to get the ugly plaid suitcase when

I remembered that Mom had hidden it from me after the earthquake. What would I have done with my clothes if I had made the bus fare to get to Cleveland? Packed them in green plastic garbage bags?

"Where's the suitcase, Mom?" I called.

"It's in my bedroom closet." Mom appeared in the hall. "But don't you want to see what I bought you?"

"Can't I look at it later? I want to pack."

Mom felt my forehead. "You must be ill. You've never stayed away from a closed shopping bag before."

"Mom!"

"Tell you what. You can get the suitcase out of my room and then meet me back in the living room before you pack. That's the best compromise I can offer."

"Oh, okay," I sighed. I went into Mom's bedroom and dragged the suitcase into my room, where I plunked it onto my bed. Then I walked back into the living room.

"All right, I'm here. What did you get me?" I plopped on the couch next to the packages. I opened a bag bulging with promise and peered in. "Gee — socks."

"And underwear."

"Wow!" I whistled. I opened another bag. "And a plain white shirt. Impressive. Thanks, Mom."

But I really did appreciate it, so I leaned over and kissed her cheek.

"Open the yellow bag," Josh said.

I opened it. It looked like pajamas. When I touched it I realized it was a sweatshirt. I pulled it out of the bag and held it up by the shoulders. I stared at a cartoon reindeer wearing sunglasses and carrying a surfboard. *Have a totally gnarly Christmas, dude*, it said across the chest.

Mom knew I hated California surfer slang, so I knew I had Josh to thank for the sweatshirt. But I didn't know quite what to say. I looked at the shirt again. Maybe I could wear it for taking out the garbage.

"I thought you might want to wear that while you're in Cleveland so people would know you're from L.A.," Josh said.

"Isn't it darling?" Mom stood behind Josh smiling a "you'd-better-say-the-right-thing" smile.

"It's absolutely, uh, *rad*, Josh. It's great. I'll wear it, 'fer sure.' " Maybe when I cleaned the bathtub.

"I'm glad." Josh smiled. Mom smiled. I had said the right thing.

"Mom, are you going to help me pack?" I stuffed the sweatshirt deep down into the bag.

"No. I thought Josh could help you. I wanted to take a shower before we all go out tonight."

"Out?"

"Josh is going to take us to El Coyote for Mexican food."

"You know, as a bon voyage," Josh added.

"You mean you're not cooking the last night I'm home?" I was disappointed. I had expected meat loaf, mashed potatoes, and chocolate cake with white icing for my sendoff. Now that Mom worked all day for somebody else I hardly ever got her to make my favorite. "I was all set for meat loaf."

"But sweetie, you probably won't get Mexican food in Cleveland."

"Well, big—"

"Philip, maybe I will help you pack after all." Before I could even close my mouth, Mom put her arm around my shoulders and whisked me off to the bedroom.

When we got there she turned to me and hissed, "Philip, what is wrong with you? Josh just bought you a sweatshirt for your trip."

"Yeah, it was really bad, if you know what I mean."

"Stop that! Josh didn't have to buy you anything."

"Sure he did."

"What do you mean?"

"He's taking you on a trip, right?"

"So?"

"Well, he doesn't think I'll let you go with him on a trip for nothing, does he?" I unzipped the suitcase and peered under the flap. Mom's laugh surprised me enough to bring me out again. "What's so funny?"

"Oh, that's just so cute, what you said."

"Yeah, right. Ha, ha. Laugh, but you know I'm telling the truth."

Mom sat down on the bed and wiped a tear from her eye. "Listen. Two things. First, I should hope I'm worth more than a sweatshirt, even a designer one. And second, Josh isn't buying me from you. Philip, it was my decision to go. If the trip still upsets you, let's discuss it. But don't make out that Josh is buying affection from either of us. Lorsches cannot be bought."

"Sorry." I turned my back and took some Levi's from the closet.

"Phil?" Mom came and stood behind me. She stroked the hair off my forehead. "Don't be angry at me."

"I'm not. I'm okay. You're right, that was a pretty dumb thing for me to say." I tossed my jeans on the bed. "Have you seen my snowflake ski sweater?"

"You're sure you don't want to talk some more?"

"I'm sure." We'd had enough talks over the past year and a half to last a lifetime.

"Okay, your choice. Um, your sweater? Isn't it in the box on the top shelf of your closet?"

I got a chair and hopped up to look. "It's here, with a million other sweaters I never get to wear."

"Then aren't you lucky you'll get a chance to wear them now?"

"I'll say. I'm sick of spring clothes. I can't wait to

put on gloves." I slapped a pair against my palm and tossed them on the bed, too.

"And you'll get to drink hot cider when you come in from the snow."

"And sleep under one of Grandma's down quilts." I pitched two wool hats onto the bed.

"And walk in crunchy snow with your boots on."

"And make a snow fort." I threw down my thick gray muffler. I dug around in the closet some more. My hand felt something fuzzy. I pulled. I stared down at something that had once been familiar. "Look! Earmuffs!"

I put them on and danced on the chair. Mom laughed. She came over and wrapped a muffler around my neck. Then she pulled one of my wool hats over the top of my head. I kept dancing. Man, I couldn't wait to see snow.

"Did you see the paper this morning, Mom?" I shouted as I danced. "Twenty-eight degrees. It's just got to snow any day now."

"It better!" Mom yelled back.

"Earmuffs! No wonder you didn't hear the phone ring." Josh was standing in the doorway. I stopped dancing immediately. "What's going on in here?"

"Nothing," I told him, not wanting to let him in on the fun Mom and I were having together.

"Oh." He turned to Mom. "Well, your mother's on the phone."

"Is she? Gee, I guess I didn't hear the phone either." She threw down a sweater she'd been holding and hurried out of my room.

"So," Josh said, looking around. "Do you have a lot to pack? Can I do something to help?"

"Not really." I took off my hat and earmuffs. "I'm just packing some old sweaters and junk. I think it's under control."

I stepped down from the chair and unzipped my parka from its hanger. It looked lonely. I held out the black and magenta jacket to admire it. I had only worn it one winter.

"Guess you'll need that where you're going."

What an observant guy. "Well, I'm sure never going to use it here."

"You know, you could be wrong about that."

"How's that?"

"Well, you haven't really seen much of California yet. Take the desert, for example. It's hot enough to fry an egg on a rock during the day and cold enough to freeze water at night. And it snows in the Sierras, you know."

"Huh." I had to admit the thought of snow anywhere in California amazed me. "How far is it? To the snow, I mean?"

"Oh, I don't know. I think it's about eight hours to, say, Mammoth Lakes."

"Eight hours? People actually drive eight hours just to go to the snow?"

Josh grinned. "You're going twenty-five hundred miles, aren't you? Just to see snow?"

"That's different."

"Philip?" We both turned as Mom came back into the room. Her eyes looked worried. "It's about your trip."

Mom sat down on the bed. My stomach sank. I was pretty sure I already knew what was about to happen.

14

"**G**randma had a fall this morning," Mom said evenly. "There was ice on the steps, and she slipped and sprained her ankle."

"Is she okay?" I did my best to sound concerned about Grandma instead of myself. "Is she in the hospital?"

"No, she and Grandpa just got back from the emergency room, but she has to stay off her feet completely for at least a week. Aunt Meryl is over there helping out."

"Why do they need Aunt Meryl if I'm coming?"

"Oh, honey. You can't take care of Grandma. Grandma still has to take care of you." My mother patted the space next to her on the bed. "Sit down, Philip."

"No, I'm okay." I crossed my arms, prepared to hear the worst.

She sighed. "All right, then. Listen, I'm afraid this means you'll have to postpone your trip."

"I knew it! I knew it!" I pounded my fists on my legs. "Why did this have to happen now?"

"That's not the point. It should never happen, but it did."

"But I don't understand why I can't still go. I'm sure I could help out."

"I know you'd try to help. But you know Grandpa has trouble with his eyes, and sometimes it's tiring to have someone else around when you're not feeling well."

"I promise I won't bother anybody!"

"You'd be bored."

"No, I won't. I'll be busy helping Grandma."

"You're not listening. Aunt Meryl came up from Canton to take care of her. Besides, you can go to Cleveland over Easter."

"I don't want to go over Easter. I want to go tomorrow." I frantically searched my brain for ideas. "I know! What if I went to stay with Cousin Jim and his wife? They won't mind."

"He's a retailer, Philip," Mom patiently explained. "This is his busy time of year. I can't even ask him."

"What about calling Brian's mom and asking if I could stay there? I know his mom would let me."

"You know, she probably would, but don't they visit their family in Toronto every year?"

"Oh, that's right," I moaned. I sank onto the bed next to Mom.

"I'm afraid it's a bad time of year to impose on anyone. You'll have to wait until spring."

"But the snow will be gone! I'll have a whole winter without snow!" I wanted to curse, but I picked up my gloves instead and threw them against the wall. "I don't believe it! First the earthquake and now this. Nothing good ever happens to me."

"Now that's just not true!"

"Philip, come on," Josh butted in. "You're going to have to adjust if you're going to get by in this world."

"Adjust!" I shoved my finger into my chest. "Me, adjust? That's a joke. I always have to 'adjust' to everything around here. Everybody else just pretends everything's okay all the time. I don't see them having to adjust. So don't talk to me about adjusting. I'm an expert!"

"Now look here! I won't—"

"Amy, leave him alone already."

"Josh—"

"Look at him. He's angry and upset. What are you going to accomplish by talking to him now?"

Mom's mouth closed. She looked at me hard for a moment. Then she got up and stood next to Josh. "Maybe you're right. Philip and I will talk when we've both calmed down. Philip, I think we'll just leave you alone for now." The two of them walked out of the room, shutting the door quietly behind them.

That was definitely not what I wanted to hear. I wanted to hear the door slam—WHAM! I was tempted to open the door and do the job for them, but that would only bring Mom running. I couldn't face talking to her now.

I rushed over and slapped off the light. I stood and listened to my angry breathing in the darkness. Not going! *Not going!* I closed my eyes and tried to make myself feel better by looking again at the happy midwestern scenes I had created in my mind to get through the waiting. Nothing. My mind's pictures had shrunk and disappeared like snow-puddles in spring.

Not that I blamed Grandma for not wanting me around. I was just a lot of trouble for both my grandparents, since they insisted on doing everything for me. They spoiled me, and I missed that, too. Poor Grandma. No wonder she wanted Aunt Meryl there and not me. I imagined her sitting in a chair with her ankle all bandaged up. I wondered if she was sad that I wasn't coming. I'd have to call her, but later.

For now, all I could do was flop down on the bed and cry.

I don't know how much time passed before Mom tapped on the door and woke me up.

"Philip?" The door opened slowly. "Are you awake?"

"I am now." I sat up in bed.

"Can I turn on the light? I want to talk to you."

"What about?" The light went on. I put a hand up to shield my eyes.

"Josh and I thought we might all take the trip up the coast together. That way you'd still get a break from the city and get to see some other parts of the state."

"Is that supposed to help me 'adjust' or something?"

"You could think of it that way." Josh had come into the room, too.

"Come on," Mom wheedled. "It'll be great to take a vacation together. We haven't traveled anywhere special for a long time."

A trip to the dentist would have been more welcome—at least I'd get a free toothbrush. I felt hurt she would even suggest such a thing after what I had been through earlier in the evening. Besides, I just didn't feel right about the three of us together on vacation, like a little family or something.

All of a sudden, I knew. That was exactly what Josh wanted. And probably what Mom wanted, too. See what I mean about having to do all the adjusting?

"No way, Mom. I'm not going with you. Forget it."

"Oh, come on, Philip. It'll be fun," Josh said. "We'll go see the aquarium in Monterey."

"And we'll visit Hearst Castle."

"And Big Sur. You'll like Big Sur, I'm sure." Josh laughed at his stupid rhyme.

"No, it's okay." I sat up on the bed. "I'd rather stay here with Bernice."

"But Bernice—" Mom started.

"Phil, you must be kidding," Josh blurted. "Why don't you want to come with us?"

"And break up your little honeymoon? No, thank you. I'd rather stay here and eat cookies."

"Honeymoon? What are you talking about?" Mom sputtered. "Josh and I aren't getting married."

"Is that what's bothering you?" Josh sounded amused. "You and your mom will stay together. Right, Amy? At least that's what I assumed."

"I said no," I told them both. "I don't want to go. I'll just stay here. It's not that big a deal. I won't be lonely. Washington will be here. I have my cats to play with. Who'd feed them if I left, anyway? Which reminds me." I stood up and moved toward the door.

"Philip, no. Wait." Mom gently put a hand on my shoulder. "Think carefully for a second. Postponing your trip to Cleveland doesn't have to spoil your whole vacation."

"No, just my whole life."

"You're being ridiculous."

"Maybe to you."

"All right, then, your life is ruined. You're ten years old and it's over. That's all right. You can even blame me if you want. But come along with us anyway. Maybe you'll change your mind and have a good time after all."

"I doubt it."

"Look, you do have a choice," Mom continued. "You can come with us and see some beautiful new places or you can stay here in Hollywood and stew in your misery."

"Some choice."

"You set it up." Mom shrugged. "You decide."

I leaned until my head thunked on the wall. There was a third, stronger possibility. I could go on the trip *and* be completely miserable. But at least if I went on the trip I'd get out of L.A. That alone was worth the price of admission.

"Okay, I'll go. Anything to get out of here for a few days." If I was lucky I might even get that free toothbrush out of the deal.

"Good. I'm glad." Mom reached out and squeezed my shoulders.

"We're both glad," Josh added. "You know, I just

thought of something. Why don't we ask your friend Washington to come along?"

"Josh, that's a great idea. What do you think, Philip?"

How could I stew in misery if Washington came? And how could I say no to their offer? I'd been cranky enough for three lifetimes and couldn't afford four. Mom and Josh were doing their best to make me feel better, even if it was hard to admit it was working.

"Yeah, sure, whatever," I said grudgingly.

"Wonderful. I'll go call his mother right now." Mom bustled off to use the bedroom phone.

"Right, sure. Make it one big party." I got up and reached for my Akron U. sweatshirt as I brushed by Josh. "I'm going to run down and feed the cats. At least somebody's going to get dinner around here."

"All right." Josh laughed. "Maybe we'll just have to call for a pizza tonight."

The elevator smelled like wet dog. I ran outside and rattled the box of cat food in my hand.

"Jumbo! Wilson! Petunia!" Shake, shake, shake. "Guys?"

"Mwow!"

"Jumbo! It's you." I poured food into the paper plate on the front steps. "You're just the cat I was looking for."

I sat down and left him alone for a few minutes so

he could eat. Then he came over and bumped the top of his head on my knee.

"Jumbo." I pulled the cat onto my lap. I didn't normally speak aloud to the strays, but I badly needed to talk. "You won't believe what just happened to me. I found out that I'm not going to get to see snow in Cleveland after all. How's that for disaster prediction?"

Jumbo licked my face. I sniffed his fur. He smelled cool and dusty.

"I feel really bad about Grandma. But I don't want to stay here. And I don't really want to go with Mom and Josh, either. I'm sure they don't want me along, anyway. They're just being understanding. Besides, who wants to go up the crummy old coast anyway?"

"Yahoo!" Washington whooped as he leaped through the Nirvana's front door. Jumbo jumped out of my arms and ran away as Washington came to a slam-footed stop in front of me.

"My mom said I could go! Aren't you glad? I've always wanted to go up to Monterey. This is going to be great, isn't it?"

"Not as great as Cleveland."

"Oh. Well, maybe not for you. Hey, I'm sorry about your grandmother."

"Thanks."

"Your mom invited me to have pizza with you."

"Great."

"So what's wrong with you?"

"Nothing." I couldn't expect other people to keep up with all my troubles. "Like I said, great. Everything is just . . . just great. Come on, let's go."

I'd pretend to enjoy the pizza. I'd pretend to enjoy the trip. I'd pretend just the way I was supposed to pretend everything. To show how well "adjusted" I was.

15

"I'm boiling." I used my sleeve to wipe my forehead as I walked down the front steps of the Nirvana with my suitcase.

"Then take off your sweater," Mom suggested.

"No, I don't want to." It was winter and I was going to wear a sweater. If I couldn't wear my snowflake sweater in Cleveland I'd just have to wear it in California.

I handed Josh my suitcase and watched him place it in the trunk of his huge green Coupe de Ville. He started to slam the trunk closed, then stopped, saying, "Oh, good, here comes Washington."

I looked up the sidewalk. Washington could not be missed. He wore an unbelievable Hawaiian shirt decorated with surfing Santas which he had tucked into a pair of red pants. On his nose sat a pair of wraparound red shades.

"What are you supposed to be?" I asked him. "Supertourist?"

"You think *I'm* dressed weird? What about you? Why are you wearing a sweater?"

"Why?" I tried to think of some smart answer, but all I could come up with was, "What's it to you?"

Washington shrugged and handed his red duffle bag to Josh. Then he looked at my mom and asked, "Are all the kids in Cleveland this weird?"

Mom laughed. "Just the ones who have to miss the snow. Right, Philip?"

I shrugged. "I guess."

"All right, everyone. Enough!" commanded Josh. "Let's get in and get rolling before all the other Sunday drivers clog the freeway."

Washington must have sensed that I didn't feel like talking, so we rode in silence in the back seat while Mom and Josh chit-chatted. The Coupe de Ville sputtered along the Hollywood Freeway, which turned into the Ventura Freeway, which passed under the San Diego Freeway and eventually led to Pacific Coast Highway. I found myself sliding down in my seat every time I saw somebody pointing at the sharp, wide fins on the rear of Josh's car.

"Look at the ocean, Philip," Mom shouted excitedly as it came into view.

"Yeah, we can pretend it's a pool of melted

snow." No response. Either no one heard or no one got my joke.

We got to Santa Barbara after an hour and a half. Josh pulled off the highway and headed up one of the rounded brown hills. He parked the Caddy between two smelly tour buses and we piled out to stretch. Josh pointed at a huge, old white church topped with curved red tiles.

"There it is," Josh said proudly, like he had something to do with the building's very existence. "Queen of the Missions."

"It's really lovely," Mom said.

"It looks a lot bigger than the pictures I've seen in school," Washington added.

I crossed my arms and waited while Josh dropped money in the donation box. The inside of the building was cool. The temperature, I mean. Josh had already explained that the adobe bricks the Indians had made to build the mission kept out the sun's heat. I felt smug about wearing my sweater now.

We walked through rooms filled with old furniture. It wasn't the kind Dad bought in Europe, which was carved and fancy. This furniture was very flat and plain. Mom studied it all carefully, storing up ideas for the day she became a set designer. Mrs. Trundle had taught us a lot about California Indians, especially the local Chumash tribe, but she hadn't said anything about what Josh now told us.

"The Spaniards built the missions as bases for

converting the Indians to Catholicism," Josh said as we walked into the cemetery with its worn tombstones and cool green garden. Oh, no. I had forgotten that Josh was a professor. Were we bound for a lecture at every stop? Josh went on, "But the Indians weren't used to being around anybody except other Indians. They caught diseases from the Spaniards and a lot of them died. Some died because they just weren't able to adapt to a new life."

This last point was obviously directed at me. I stared ahead at a wooden grave marker and muttered under my breath, "Others died from boring lectures."

"What?" Josh asked.

"Nothing."

"Oh." Josh looked at me with doubt for a moment. Then, to my dismay, he took a deep breath and continued. "You know, there were once Indians living out on those islands we saw as we drove up the coast." We followed Josh back into the church. "There's a story about a girl who lived on San Nicolas Island by herself for many years."

"Really? All alone?" Washington asked.

"Right. The book is called *Island of the Blue Dolphins*. You should read it. The girl in the story gets left alone on the island. She has to learn how to cook, hunt, make clothes—to survive with no one to help."

I had to admit that sounded impressive, but I

didn't comment. I listened to Wash and Josh yak until we got back to the car.

We climbed into the Coupe de Ville which now completely stank of diesel fuel. I coughed a protest. Nobody listened.

"Next stop, Morro Bay!" Josh bellowed like a conductor as we whipped around the freeway on-ramp, tires squealing. "I can taste those fried abalone strips already."

"Josh, slow down," Mom pleaded.

"Sorry. Abalone inspires me."

Somehow I wasn't surprised that Josh would want to eat something that was bound to taste like the Coupe de Ville's tires. Then I became truly concerned. Did Josh plan to have us try every weird West Coast food he could find on our trip? I made a note to keep my eyes peeled for the golden arches or the Colonel's friendly face as we made our way to Morro Bay.

16

Morro Bay turned out to be an old fishing town. The scenic highlight, Bird Rock, sat like a giant in the center of the bay. And that's all it did. Sat.

"Look at the beautiful color of these pebbles," Mom said as we walked across the beach.

"Really great, Mom." I took off my shoe and poured several of the beautiful pebbles back onto the sand. I looked at Washington to see if he got the joke. To my surprise he was standing and staring, awe-struck, at Bird Rock.

"How do you think that rock got out there?" he asked.

"Well, you see, there was this millionaire who lived up over there," Josh began, sounding like a professor again. "His favorite way to relax was to stand at his window and watch the sun set into the ocean. But there was an obstacle to his pleasure."

"What was that?" Washington asked with a smile.

"The sun. It hurt his eyes. So he had the poor fellows who worked for him get a bunch of ropes and tug that big rock down from that hill right into the sea."

"For real?" I asked. Now this was impressive. "How many guys did it take?" No one said anything. I saw a look pass between Josh and Washington. "What's the matter? I asked a question, that's all."

Mom and Washington burst out laughing. Then Josh joined in with a sputter. The three of them could have been a family sharing a good joke. I felt confused. I didn't want to be part of their cozy little group, but now I felt left out.

"Philip, you can be such a dope," Washington said once he stopped laughing.

Washington's comment was more than I could stand. "Shut up! Shut up! I knew it was a joke! I'm not that stupid."

"We know that," Mom said. "Calm down."

"Anyway, nobody really knows how it got there," Josh went on. "That's the whole mystery of the rock."

That wasn't enough to make it interesting. The rock just sat there dumbly while the people on the beach sat there and watched it, equally dumb. Then I noticed another possible mystery.

"What's that white stuff all over it?" I asked. I was sorry as soon as I opened my mouth.

Josh grinned. "Well, there are a million birds on that rock out there. Want to take a guess as to what it is?"

"Oh, gross!" I wrinkled my nose and turned away. "Forget I asked."

"Oh, look! A seal!" Mom shouted. "See him?"

"Ooops, there he goes!" Josh said.

Which meant I turned around just in time to see . . . nothing. "Where'd he go? I don't see anything."

"Weren't you watching?" Washington sounded annoyed. "Why are you so out of it?"

"I'm not out of it. Anyway, maybe there wasn't any dumb seal. Maybe it was just—"

"Philip!" Mom cried. "Enough!"

"Maybe we're all hungry." Josh clapped his hands together. "Let's go get some abalone."

"Can't we just get a hamburger?" Nobody heard me. I muttered again louder. "All I want is a plain old hamburger."

"Don't be a nerd," Washington said. "You can get a hamburger any time."

"Not in abalone country," I grumbled.

Or more to the point, not in baloney country. And someone here was full of it.

"Look at this cute little place," Mom exclaimed as we drove up to Chuck's Abalone House. The house was more like a dingy white hut, with limp

115

curtains hanging in the windows. Flies buzzed around the screen door, as anxious as Josh for a taste of abalone. Mom would never have let us eat in a place like this. Amazing how love blinded people, even mothers.

We sat down at a table topped with an abalone shell ashtray and big, plain salt and pepper shakers. I picked up the salt shaker for a closer look.

"What's the rice for?" I asked.

"It gets damp here. They put that in to keep the salt flowing," Josh said. He smiled. "My mother had to do the same thing when I was growing up in Redondo Beach."

"You lived in Redondo Beach?" Washington asked. "Do you know how to surf?"

"Not on a board, just body surfing."

"Cool." Wash and Josh were at it again, Washington wanting to know all about Josh's glory days at the beach.

I opened the menu the waiter had left. It smelled of oil. Abalone this and abalone that. My eyes bugged. "Do you know how many quarter pounders we could buy for what this abalone costs?"

"That's why it's such a special treat," Mom explained.

Which only made me more leery. Why is it when an adult says something's a treat it usually isn't?

The waiter showed up and took three orders for fried abalone strips in a basket, then looked at me. I squirmed in my chair, then asked, "Do you have any hamburgers?"

The waiter laughed. I hated it when waiters laughed at me. "No, but we have peanut butter."

I hated peanut butter, too. But on principle I said, "That's what I'll have, then. Peanut butter and jelly, please."

The waiter soon came back with three baskets of deep-fried, breaded abalone strips next to piles of golden, greasy french fries. Josh, Wash, and Mom hooked their nostrils on the steam rising from their food. Even my mouth watered, the traitor.

Then the waiter plopped a small white plate in front of me. Purple jelly blobbed out from under the white bread, bread which was forbidden in our house. Mom ignored my look of disgust and dove into her food.

"I've been waiting for this ever since we started planning our trip." Josh speared an abalone strip with his fork and munched. "Aaaah—Neptune must have eaten this, food for the gods."

I bit into my peanut butter. I felt like Charlie Brown in those old cartoon books where the peanut butter sticks to the roof of his mouth and makes him feel worse than he already feels.

"This is great." Washington looked at me, his eyes sympathetic. "You want to try a piece?"

"No, thanks," I managed to say through my peanut butter.

"You sure?" Mom asked, waving a piece of fried abalone on her fork.

I shrugged. What could I lose? If it was gross I could always spit it out and act like I was dying. "Okay."

Mom let me take her fork. I had expected abalone to be rubbery, but it wasn't at all. It was tender, soft, juicy. Delicious. I felt like a jerk.

"How is it?" Mom asked.

"All right." It was more than all right, but how could I admit my mistake?

I looked down at my half-eaten sandwich, remembering something that happened when I was a little kid. I was going to have this big birthday party and had asked Grandma for a chocolate cake. For some reason Grandma got mixed up and baked vanilla instead. I thought my whole party would be wrecked, and when everyone got there I acted like such a brat that it was just about ruined.

But what was worse was that my friends all loved the cake, which Grandma had decorated like a fire truck. I finally gave in and had a piece. It's still the best birthday cake I've ever had.

All I had done was spoil my own party over something completely dumb.

Clank!

My sandwich plate had fallen on the floor, bringing me back to Chuck's.

"Oh, no!" I stooped under the table to get it. There was peanut butter stuck to the floor.

"It's okay." The waiter rushed over with a wet cloth, then asked, "Should I get you another sandwich?"

"No. Bring him an order of abalone instead," Josh told him. I looked up, surprised. "That's what you want, isn't it?"

"Yes, I guess," I managed.

"That's what I thought," Josh said. I looked over, expecting to see a smug expression. Instead, there was a smile of genuine understanding on his face.

"Right away." The waiter walked off smiling.

Talk about weird. I sat and watched Josh eat the last of his abalone and start on his fries. For the first time I had an idea why Mom liked him.

He was easy to be around.

Unlike some people we know.

Ahem.

17

The rest of the vacation went better, but not great. We were still in California, after all. We kept doing all these cute California things, too, like eating breakfast in an omelette parlor the last morning of our trip. Mom said the place had too much charm to miss it. Everybody else refused to eat even one little meal under those famed golden arches I kept looking for.

"Asparagus omelettes for everyone!" Josh told the curly-haired waitress.

"But I've never had asparagus," I protested.

"You never had abalone, either," Josh reminded me, "and you loved it."

That was the problem. Once you allowed yourself to try one new thing, everybody expected you to become open-minded.

When the eggs came, I gritted my teeth and dug into the asparagus. It wasn't bad. Mom, Josh and

Washington kept heaping praise on the stuff. To be honest, I couldn't understand all that adoration being wasted on a slimy green vegetable.

But then, I couldn't understand why the three of them liked a lot of things we'd seen. Like Hearst Castle. Sure, some rich newspaper guy built it, but now it was kind of old and smelly, like the elevator at the Nirvana. Of course, Mom-the-future-set-designer went whacko when she saw all the over-decorated rooms. And while I liked the scenery at Big Sur, the hippies in their sixties clothing almost ruined it for me. Seeing them in their bell bottoms proved that California was the last place on Earth to have walking fossils.

The night we spent in Big Sur was also the night we had curried tofu burritos. Asparagus was weird enough, but it was a lot better than those burritos.

"What time are we leaving for L.A.?" I asked, trying to cut the stringy vegetable with the side of my fork.

"About noon," Josh said. "I thought we'd go see some tidepools first."

"Didn't we see starfish and stuff at the Monterey Aquarium yesterday?" Washington asked. He'd been rubbing his eyes all through breakfast. He and Josh had stayed up late in their room watching *Godzilla*, which I thought was hokey but Josh had insisted was a classic. Why couldn't we have watched

High Noon instead? That had hurt. It made me feel like the only Indians fan at a Dodger game. Even Mom was surprised when I came back into our room at eight and turned in for the night. "I guess I'm kind of tired," Washington said. "I could use a nap."

"But I thought you'd want to see the real thing." Josh sounded disappointed.

"Washington really looks tired," Mom said. "Frankly, I wouldn't mind going back to the motel and resting awhile myself. Then maybe we can finish up our Christmas shopping later in Carmel."

Josh didn't say anything but he looked upset as he poured sugar in his coffee.

"Why don't you just go with Philip?" Mom suggested.

I looked at Mom with bug eyes. Go with Josh alone? All I could think of to say was, "Huh?"

"Hey, what do you think, Phil? Are you up for some tidepools?" Josh seemed eager for my company.

As with the sweatshirt Josh had given me (which I had managed not to wear), I knew I would seem ungrateful if I didn't say yes. I shot Mom a look meant to remind her that Christmas was coming in just two days and that I'd better be earning points toward my presents. "Yeah, I guess."

"Then it's set," Mom said. "Philip, finish up that

asparagus. It won't be in the stores fresh until spring."

I ignored her. I turned to Washington and asked, "Are you sure you don't want to come?"

"I'm sure," he answered with a yawn.

"Look, Philip, if you don't want—" Josh began.

"No, no. I'm going, I'm going. I want to go." I even ate my last bite of asparagus to show what an easygoing kind of kid I was.

This little trip could get strange, though, I reflected once I was back in the car. The only alone time I'd ever spent with Josh had been in the elevator between floors at the Nirvana. We seemed to tolerate each other, the way you tolerate pickles on your friend's breath. You don't like it, but you put up with it.

After we dropped Mom and Washington back at the motel, Josh and I headed north up the coast in the green tank. Sitting in the front seat, I felt like I was buckled into a couch. We rode along in silence for a few minutes. Suddenly I lurched as Josh pulled across the highway onto a patch of dirt barely wide enough for the Cadillac.

"If I remember, there's a path right here to some really great pools," he told me. "Looks like the tide's out, too—that's good."

I followed behind Josh, slipping and sliding down the gravel as if my shoes had marble soles. It was embarrassing, but at least Josh didn't try to grab my hand to help. He just watched me make my own way down the hill. Then we walked down to where the ocean met the rocks.

"Careful, here. Don't get your shoes—oh, no."

Too late. I had put my foot right down into an ocean pool. "Damn."

Josh laughed.

"Damn!" I said again, looking at my wet running shoes.

"Hey, once is okay, but not twice. Anyway, it's only water. It'll dry." I opened my mouth to apologize, but Josh walked on. "Here. Come here and look at this starfish."

I picked my way across the rocks to the pool into which Josh was staring. There was a golden starfish making its way from one side of the pool to the other. Its arms waved gracefully, timidly, making me think of a blind man walking with a cane.

"It's like watching a blind dancer," I said.

"A blind dancer? That's nice." Josh grinned. "But actually, there's an eye on the end of each arm."

"I didn't know that." I crouched down to get a closer look at the little critters in the pool. There were lots of gray and purple shells, some blobby green things with what looked like colored pebbles stuck to them, and a bunch of round, purple animals covered with long spikes.

"What are those?"

"The purple ones? Urchins."

"They look poisonous. Are they?"

"Just the spikes. People eat the insides as a delicacy. Sometimes they have it at the sushi bar I like to go to."

"Gross." I wrinkled my nose. "That's one thing I'll definitely never try."

Josh snorted. "You're not really into trying new things, are you?"

I scowled. "Yes, I am."

"You can't fool me. I saw you forcing down that asparagus."

"It was delicious," I lied.

"You did eat the abalone, I guess. Oh, look, here's one."

"One what?"

"An abalone. See, the shell's kind of ugly outside. Hard to believe what it looks like when you turn it over, if you could pry it off the rock."

"Speaking of ugly, what are these green things?"

"These?" Josh put his hand into the water. I cringed as he touched one. The animal cringed, too, pulling itself into a tight knot.

"That's weird."

"It's an anemone."

I reached into the water and took a quick poke at a little one with my fingertip. This one, too, shrank in on itself, now looking more like a rock than an animal.

"Why do they do that?"

"Well, for one thing, it keeps them wet inside when the tide goes out. And for another, they have to protect themselves. They're pretty soft, but when they pull in like that they become like a big mouthful of shells for predators."

Josh became quiet. I could feel him watching me. I kept my eyes focused on the animals in the pool. I had a feeling I was in for some more of Josh's wisdom. The funny thing was, this time I wanted to listen.

Josh began speaking softly. "Some people pull in, too. For protection. You've been pretty quiet these past few days."

"I guess." I found an anemone on a different rock and gave it a poke. The waves hissed nearer.

"You know, Philip, your mom actually moved out here because of you."

I sat stone still and looked back at the first rock. The starfish had disappeared without my seeing it go.

"She once told me you seemed so sad after your dad left that she thought a change would be good for you."

"But I liked Cleveland. I liked living with my grandmother."

"Mmmm." Josh picked up a shell out of the pool. He examined it and handed it to me. "Hermit crab."

It waved its legs in my face and I pulled back. "Is

this the kind that changes shells when it outgrows the old one?"

"That's right."

Water ran into the pool in little rivulets now. The anemones opened up again. A new sea urchin came to take up residence in the pool. Little fish darted in and out from a hole in the rocks at the pool's bottom. They looked as if they were searching for their shadows.

"Everything changes." I swirled my finger in the water. "That's what you're trying to say, isn't it?"

We sat in silence and watched the sea some more.

"I don't like it when things change," I admitted.

"Why not?"

"I don't know. It hurts."

"But it doesn't have to. Look, the pools change, too, and nobody here is complaining." He pointed to a long, transparent blob floating by. "Even this poor, ugly sea cucumber."

I laughed as I thought of the anemones complaining about their living conditions: too much salt in the water, maybe. I told Josh what I had imagined and we laughed together. Then a wave whooshed over the rocks. We both sprang up and sprinted closer to the beach.

"Almost got us!" Josh said. "Want to see more? We can go farther down the beach."

"No," I answered. I looked back toward the tide-pool again for a moment. All those animals. They were so . . . adaptable. "I'm ready to go home. I mean, back to L.A."

And I was. Josh put his arm around my shoulder. I started to pull back. Then I thought of the anemone and I let his arm stay there.

For the first time I could remember, things seemed easy. I just had to adapt. Adjust. Whatever.

18

I even ate sushi. On the drive home Josh took us to his favorite sushi bar in the Valley for lunch. Okay, my favorite type was *inari* which was white rice in a plain brown wrapper—sort of a meatless wonton. They didn't have any sea urchin, but I did try a piece of octopus and I didn't gag once.

When we got back to the Nirvana, though, I still felt a little sad about celebrating my first Christmas without the possibility of snow. Even worse was the possibility of celebrating Christmas without any gifts to give out. I had been such a grinch that I hadn't done any shopping on the trip, the way everyone else had. Instead I had bought new sweat-shirts for myself at the Monterey Aquarium, one with a humpback whale and one with a sea otter on the front. I was glad that at least Mom had put some packages in the mail for our relatives back in Ohio.

I recounted the little money I still had and tried to

figure where I could go the day before Christmas to shop. Then I remembered this weird little gift store on a busy street a few blocks from the Nirvana and decided to walk over. It was sort of a dime store for rejects—the stuff, not the people. I went in and rushed up and down the aisles crowded with grouchy last-minute shoppers and cartons of wrapping paper that was already on sale.

I must have picked up and put down a hundred gifts, either because they cost too much or because they were too dumb. Finally, I found a huge fake stone pin and matching earrings for Mom and a mug with a whale on it for Josh. I got a big Santa cookie cutter for Bernice, small rawhide bones for Ping and Pong, and some mouse-shaped nummies for the cats.

For Washington, who had put up with my whining and had promised to take me skateboarding in Venice, I bought a small ukelele which had *Aloha* written in white paint across the front and a neck carved to look like a palm tree. I thought he'd look pretty cool strumming it while he sailed along on his board.

Finally, I had just enough money left to buy a stick-on deodorant for the elevator at the Nirvana and a chocolate marshmallow Santa for myself for being such a great guy.

"I'm back, Mom," I announced as I let myself into

the apartment. I was really beginning to get the Christmas spirit. "Let's go buy a tree."

"Tree?" Mom frowned.

I put my packages down on the couch and frowned back. "A Christmas tree."

"Christmas tree? You mean like a pine tree, with needles?"

I nodded.

"Didn't I tell you?" Mom gave me a grave look. "I'm going to redecorate with a Southwestern theme. Instead of a tree I thought I'd buy us a cactus. One of those big ones, you know. We can hang little silver balls from the spikes."

"Mom, no!" Some things you just didn't mess with. A Christmas tree was one of them.

"Gotcha!" Mom smiled and pinched me in the ribs. "Let's go get a tree."

I looked at colored lights as Mom drove to a lot a few blocks away. We got out and walked onto the straw-covered dirt. We stood for a moment to breathe in the rich, sweet fragrance of pine. Then we silently went off in our own directions to look for the right tree. Not too tall or too short, and full, with a good pointy shape.

Even this late on Christmas Eve there were still plenty of trees, but they slouched or had bald spots or crunchy brown needles. I crept farther and farther toward the back of the lot. For our first

Christmas in our new home this tree had to be good. Not perfect, but good.

Then I saw what looked like the best tree on the lot, at least from the front. The sides were even, with no branches too long or too short. I decided to take a look at its rear. I walked around backwards on the soft ground and bumped smack into someone— someone much larger than me. I turned around and my jaw dropped.

Miguel. Back from Mexico.

My first thought was to run off into the Christmas trees. Somehow using a Christmas tree as camouflage didn't seem right, though. So I looked straight at Miguel and said the only thing I could come up with that wasn't too dumb. "Oh. Hello."

"You?" Miguel sneered his displeasure.

"Me." I put my hands in my pockets, maybe to show "no fists," and looked around at the trees. "Funny place to run into someone."

"Especially me, right?" Miguel crossed his arms and looked down at me like a bloated spider regarding an ant.

"I guess." I felt extremely uncomfortable but I couldn't think of any way to leave. It didn't look like Miguel was going to leave either. But I couldn't just stand there staring up at him. "So. How big a tree are you getting?"

"I don't know. Small, I guess."

"Us, too. We spent all our money on a trip."

"We did, too. To go to Guadalajara."

"Wow. Guadalajara." Just the word sounded so far away that I had to know more. "Is that in Mexico?"

"Right. I went to see my dad."

"Oh. I was supposed to go to Ohio. To see my family, but it didn't work out."

Miguel looked away. "Neither did mine."

"Oh." I never would have guessed we had anything in common. Now I was really curious. "Why didn't it work out?"

"I didn't want to stay with my dad after all. Things are pretty bad down there. The house had a dirt floor and there was no plumbing. It was bad, that's all."

"So you have to stay in L.A.?"

Miguel nudged the ground with his toe. "Looks like."

Me, too, I wanted to say, but I didn't get the chance because Miguel's mom appeared. She didn't say anything, just waited for Miguel to join her. No, who's your friend? Or, aren't you going to introduce me? Then I realized that she didn't speak English. Washington was right. It must have been hard to speak one language at school and another at home.

I watched them turn and walk away together, Miguel nearly as tall as his mother. Then I thought of something.

"Miguel! Wait!" I trotted after him, pulling two quarters from my pocket.

Miguel stopped and turned around. "What is it?"

"Here." I put the quarters in his hand. "I owe these to you."

Miguel looked at the coins and frowned. "What for? I got you in trouble."

"I know. But you were right. I should have told you I was keeping them." I gulped. "I was just trying to make some money to go back and see my family early."

"I didn't know that. But I know how it is." Miguel closed his hands over the quarters and looked at me. "Hey, Lorsch, you know what?"

"What?" I asked.

For some dumb reason I expected him to thank me. Instead Miguel said, "You sure are one big dweeb."

"Gee, thanks, Miguel. I was just beginning to think you were normal, too."

Miguel scrunched up his face. "You tiny-headed—"

"Philip?"

I heard my mother's call with relief. "I've got to go." I took a deep breath and looked at Miguel's mother. Then I spoke just about the only Spanish I had learned. *"Felíz navidád."*

Her eyebrows shot up, then she smiled. *"Felíz navidád."*

I turned and walked over to the tree my mother

was looking at. I felt a tightness in my throat that I couldn't explain. I swallowed it away as I studied the huge tree.

"Can we afford that?" I asked.

"Now there's a question I never thought I'd hear from you. No, we really can't afford it. Isn't it beautiful, though?" Mom looked at me. "Who was that you were talking to?"

"Somebody from school. Miguel. He's from Mexico." But I wanted to get a tree, not talk about Miguel. "I thought I saw a nice tree back here."

As Mom followed me across the lot, a Santa walked by wearing Ray-Bans and Nikes and eating frozen yogurt. Mom and I took one look at each other and began sputtering. Then we laughed together in a way we hadn't in a long time.

When we finally stopped, Mom dabbed the corner of her eye and admitted, "You know, things like that are tough even for an L.A. convert like me."

"Oh, Mom." I reached out to feel if the tree's needles were still moist. "Get with the program."

"Get with the—huh?" She looked at me, then realized what I meant. "Oh, you mean adjust?"

I smiled and nodded. Then I pointed to the tree. "So what do you think?"

"I think . . . I think it's a great tree!"

"You know, now that I'm looking at it again it seems a little too small. But I'm not complaining!" And it was true. "It'll be fine."

"Okay, let's get it," Mom said happily. "When we get home we can make some hot chocolate and pretend it's snowing while we trim the tree."

"Why bother?" I felt peaceful looking up at the empty, dark, starless sky. "You know what? I kind of like the idea of not having to shovel the walk tomorrow morning!"

STEPHANIE JONA BUEHLER earned a BA degree from UCLA and a Master of Professional Writing degree from USC, and now teaches elementary school for the Los Angeles Unified School District. She lives in Studio City, California, with her husband, Mark, an attorney, and their daughter Anneka. *There's No Surf in Cleveland* is her first book.